PENNINGTON'S
SEVENTEENTH SUMMER

Also by K. M. Peyton:

The Beethoven Medal
Pennington's Heir

Flambards
The Edge Of the Cloud
Flambards in Summer
Flambards Divided

The Swallow Tale
The Swallow Summer
Swallow, the Star

A Pattern of Roses
The Right-Hand Man
Dear Fred
Downhill All the Way
Darkling
Firehead
Poor Badger
The Boy Who Wasn't There
The Wild Boy and Queen Moon
Windy Webley
Unquiet Spirits
The Paradise Pony
The Scruffy Pony
Pony in the Dark
Stealaway
Small Gains
Greater Gains
Blue Skies and Gunfire

PENNINGTON'S SEVENTEENTH SUMMER

K. M. Peyton

RED FOX CLASSICS

PENNINGTON'S SEVENTEENTH SUMMER
A RED FOX CLASSICS BOOK 978 1 782 95109 4

First published in Great Britain by Oxford University Press

1 3 5 7 9 10 8 6 4 2

Text copyright © K. M. Peyton, 1970

The right of K. M. Peyton to be identified as the author of this work has been
asserted in accordance with the Copyright, Designs and Patents Act 1988.

The Random House Group Limited supports The Forest Stewardship
Council® (FSC®), the leading international forest-certification organisation.
Our books carrying the FSC label are printed on FSC®-certified paper.
FSC is the only forest-certification scheme supported by the leading
environmental organisations, including Greenpeace. Our
paper procurement policy can be found at
www.randomhouse.co.uk/environment

MIX
Paper from
responsible sources
FSC® C018072

Set in Bembo 12/17pt by Falcon Oast Graphic Art Ltd.

Random House Children's Publishers UK,
61–63 Uxbridge Road, London W5 5SA

www.randomhousechildrens.co.uk
www.totallyrandombooks.co.uk
www.randomhouse.co.uk

Addresses for companies within The Random House Group Limited can be
found at: www.randomhouse.co.uk/offices.htm

THE RANDOM HOUSE GROUP Limited Reg. No. 954009

A CIP catalogue record for this book is available from the British Library.

Printed and bound in Great Britain by Clays Ltd, St Ives plc

CHAPTER ONE

PENN READ SLOWLY down his report. Apart from games – 'Excellent' – the remarks were the usual, brief and unenthusiastic: 'Poor', 'Fair', 'Could do better'. Under Mathematics it said, 'Idle and destructive in class, in spite of innate ability', and under the heading 'Extras: Music' a crabbed hand had written angrily, 'May God forgive this boy for abusing so unusual a talent.' Penn pondered this remark, scowling. Then he yawned, and passed the document to his friend, Bates.

Bates read it and said, 'Only Dotty Crocker makes any effort at all. He gave you a good one last term. How did it go?'

'"This boy plays the piano as befits the captain of the first eleven."'

'Yes. That was good.'

'A plus,' Penn agreed.

'What's Soggy said?'

Penn turned the report over to 'Character and Obedience'. '"Unsatisfactory in the extreme. It is

1

imperative that Pennington cultivates a sense of responsibility in keeping with his position in the school",' he read.

'Old enough to have more sense,' Bates translated.

'Old enough to leave,' Penn said heavily.

He certainly looked old enough to leave, a fourteen-stone hulk of a boy, with shoulders on him like an all-in wrestler, and long reddish-brown hair curling over his collar. He would, in fact, have left the year before if he had had his way, but his mother had browbeaten all the formidable male opposition – Penn himself, his father, and almost all the staff at the Beehive Secondary Modern – into subjection. She hadn't been educated herself and she wanted her boy educated, and if the inefficient bunch at the Beehive that called themselves teachers couldn't achieve it in the fifteen years prescribed by law, she was quite prepared to give them another year. All the very sincere protestations by the Beehive staff that another year wouldn't make any significant difference in the level of Penn's attainment, because the boy himself did not choose to be educated, had not persuaded her to change her mind. Only the games master had shown any joy, Penn's presence at the Beehive being the prime reason why the school held the county shields for both soccer and swimming. The eccentric music master, Mr Crocker, had kept his thoughts to himself: they were complicated thoughts of despair and frustration, lifted on occasion by moments of acute joy when Pennington chose to show what he was capable of. Mr Crocker was not prepared to discuss with anyone how Pennington caused him to suffer. All the rest of the staff would discuss the fact only too readily.

'Another year of him!' Even the headmaster, a cautious man, uttered the heresy. 'The only subject he has anything to show for in the way of attainment is music. Oh, and I believe he scraped a pass in R.E. A strange pair of passes,' he added cryptically to Penn's form master, Marsh, 'for a boy who, let's face it, is essentially a thug.'

'I've been facing it for two years now,' said Mr Marsh. And Penn was committed for another year. ('Committed' was his own word.)

On the back seat of the bus, Penn's arch-enemy, Smeeton, was lighting his report with the cigarette he was smoking. He held it up, flaming, to the admiration of all around him. Even Penn, against his will, was impressed.

'Ruddy show-off,' he said to Bates.

'He wrote a letter to his mother, two years ago, saying that reports had been abolished, and put Stacker's signature on it,' Bates said.

'Oh, he's bright,' Penn said disparagingly. Penn had broken into a sweet shop with Smeeton two years previously and stolen four Easter eggs and ten cigarettes, and he had been put on probation; no one had known about Smeeton. Penn had never forgiven Smeeton for this superior crooksmanship. Smeeton was slight, sharp-witted, greasy, and mean.

As the bus lurched into the village they piled down the stairs, Penn managing nicely to thump Smeeton off balance so that he landed heavily on top of the conductor, who swore at him very satisfactorily. The shopping women glared and said, 'It's time someone taught you yobs some manners!' They always said that. They complained to Stacker about the boys' behaviour, and their hair, and their swearing, and Stacker was very charming to them, and gave them a cup of tea, and said he'd give the boys something to remember, but when the door had closed behind the women he just went back to what he was doing before they interrupted him.

'You coming down to the boat tonight?' Penn asked Bates, before they parted. He raised his voice so that Smeeton would hear him.

'Yep. If you're going.'

'I'm going.'

'OK. See you.'

'Funny thing,' Smeeton said to Penn. 'Gerry and I

4

thought of taking the boat out tonight. His brother'll most likely come, too.'

'Amazing!' said Penn.

Satisfied by the reaction, he turned on his heel and walked home. The evening showed promise, in that short exchange. The prospect of mashing Smeeton was never less than entrancing. Penn's physical superiority was a source of constant satisfaction, for Smeeton had to collect at least three friends before he would risk a fight with Penn, and Smeeton did not come by friends easily. Penn grinned to himself, turning in at the gate of his house. The boat, an ancient fishing-smack rotting quietly away by itself on the river, provided perennial fight potential, both boys claiming ownership. Its former owner, in a confused dotage, had promised it to both boys when he died. At the time of the promise Penn and Smeeton had been on amicable terms, but the old boy had taken a long time in dying. The two boys could easily have shared ownership if they wished, neither of them particularly wanting to use it until he knew the other did, but it was a useful source of grievance, a convenient excuse for argument. Anything, Penn thought, to relieve the boredom.

Going in the back door, he remembered his report, and the gloom settled again. He dropped the battered kitbag containing his filthy soccer gear, running shoes, smelly socks and two blood-stained handkerchiefs on the floor, and made for the television set.

'Your tea's ready.' His mother waylaid him before he got out of the kitchen. 'Sit down with your father. I'm not going to stand at the cooker all night. That blazer'll have to go to the cleaner's this holidays. I don't know what you do to your clothes half the time.'

'I just wear them.'

'You got something fixed up for the holidays?' his father asked. He was sitting at the kitchen table, mopping up the remains of his dinner with a slice of bread. He had just got up, being on nights for the next three months. Penn had forgotten about the switch-round, and glowered at his father.

'There's no jobs going round here.'

'Not if you haven't asked, I dare say,' his father said sarcastically. 'What's wrong with the chicken factory?'

'I'll find something.'

'Pick this rubbish up,' his mother said. 'You got a report, or are you hiding it?'

'No.' Penn pulled the crumpled letter out of his pocket and dropped it on the table, slumping into his place opposite his father. 'It's nothing to get excited about.'

'That'll be the day,' said his father.

But Penn knew that his father boasted about his

playing centre-half for the county schools eleven, and preferred this prowess to high scores for English literature. It was not the 'poors' and 'fairs' that were going to get him into trouble, but old Dotty Crocker's broadside.

His mother put his dinner down, poured herself a cup of tea, and opened up the document. She read down it, frowning.

Penn watched her, apprehensive. His mother was Irish, with an Irish temper, a flinty, unlovable mother. She worked in a trousers factory in Northend and spent most of her wages in the betting shop. She was voluble, argumentative, and unpredictable, treating Penn according to her mood with indulgence, indifference, or gross injustice, so that in sixteen years he had never known where he stood with her. His father was easier to understand, although no easier to live with, settling all arguments by means of a good thumping. Penn's own predisposition to settle arguments by the same means was merely imitative, not a psychological Freudian aggression to be treated by the Child Guidance Clinic, as some of the more nervous pedagogues at the Beehive suggested. 'Pennington is only what his parents have made him,' suggested Mr Crocker, but nobody listened to him, and Penn had to take the blame for his nature himself.

'What's this, of Mr Crocker's?' his mother asked. 'What's he mean?'

Penn shrugged, shovelling in food.

'What's he mean? "Abusing—"? I never can understand this man.'

'I was in the bog playing my harmonica, and he heard me and waited, and when I came out he blasted off about if I spent as much time practising Bach and Co. as I did playing rubbish on a rubbishy instrument I'd be Paderewski or somebody by now. Well, that's what he meant. He didn't say it exactly.'

'Your hair's long enough,' said his father.

'We're paying good money for your lessons,' his mother said. 'They're not on the rates, like the rest of your education. You'll be sorry later on you wasted time monkeying about.'

The reaction was milder than Penn had expected. He heaved a sigh of relief and said, 'I'm going down the river.'

'You're practising first.'

'Afterwards.'

'Now. Let your dinner get down.'

Penn sighed, heavily. He pushed his plate back and wiped his mouth.

'You can see about a job, too,' his father said. 'Purvis might take you.'

'I've asked him.'

Penn escaped. He didn't want to tell his father what Purvis had said. The Easter eggs and the ten cigarettes had branded Penn, and people in the village still threw it up in his face, as if it was murder. Penn didn't care much, except when it was inconvenient, like losing him a job off old Purvis, who kept the boatyard. 'I can't afford to lose gear,' Purvis had said.

Young Jim Purvis had said, 'Oh, come off it, Dad. Pat wouldn't touch anything here.'

'I'm not employing Patrick Pennington,' old Purvis had reiterated.

Penn went upstairs and changed into jeans and a denim shirt. He dropped his school clothes in a heap on the floor, combed his hair carefully, and examined the one or two spots on his face in the mirror. He put the harmonica that lay on the chest of drawers into his back pocket, and went downstairs to the front room, where the piano was.

'Mrs Jones, here I come,' he muttered, and played a chord that shook everything in the room. Mrs Jones lived next door, and had hammered on the wall so often that Penn thought she would soon be right through. He sat slumped, looking down at his hands, thinking about a job. The boatyard would have been all right. A bit of humping gear and slapping on the old paint. His hands were enormous, the nails broken and grimy, an old soccer scar across the knuckles. But from the wide, thick palms the fingers tapered, long and agile, altogether out of keeping with the rest of his bulk. These were the fingers that old Crocker drove and nagged at and kept flickering up and down the keys in obedience to knotty exercises devised by Czerny and Clementi, the fingers that lapsed, as soon as his back was turned, into the current number one in the charts, or Penn's personal jazz rendering of 'Down by the Riverside'.

'Extraordinary technical brilliance, yes,' said Mr Marsh to Mr Crocker. 'Intellect to give it meaning, no.'

'I know the boy is in the C stream,' Crocker said. 'But not because he's dim. He's by no means dim—'

'He's in the C stream because he's infernally lazy, lacks any kind of responsibility or self-discipline and is bloody-minded into the bargain,' said Marsh – whom the boys called Soggy.

'Given those parents, hardly to be wondered at,' Matthews, the games master, put in quietly.

'A born troublemaker,' Soggy said.

'Phenomenal hands,' Crocker said. 'Stretch a tenth without trying, strongest fingers I've ever come across. I never cease to wonder at such talent coming from such a background.'

'Well, how come?' queried Matthews. 'I thought

pianists had to start at the age of three, or something?'

'But he did, that's the amazing thing. That ghastly mother of his, give her her due, started him on the piano – God knows why – I suppose she has some fiddling. Irish ancestors back in the Sligo bog somewhere and considers herself musical – found he was a natural, and actually kept him at it. Got an old dragon of a church harmonium player to teach him. I looked this dragon up once, out of curiosity. She said he was a sweet little boy – get that, Marsh – but by the age of about ten he was getting out of hand fast, and she gave him up because he was – well, the Pennington we know, I suppose. I know how she felt, because I've given him up a dozen times myself. But it's a wicked waste, enough to make a man weep.'

'Pennington,' said Soggy finally, 'will never – I repeat, never – get any sympathy from me.'

Quite aware of, but indifferent to, the opinions of his teachers, parents, neighbours, and passing acquaintances, Penn played the piano when compelled to, but not otherwise. He now pursued a fluent but joyless path through the three movements of a Mozart sonata, a Chopin Polonaise, and a piece by Prokofiev, then started on a rave number, which set Mrs Jones off with her poker. Glad of an excuse to give up, Penn ducked out through the kitchen, ignoring his mother's rebukes, framing silent, suitable words for her under his breath.

Once in the open, away from his natural enemies, he felt better. He tossed back his hair and started to whistle 'The Butcher Boy'. Good for old Smeeton, he thought, game for a bit of turbulence . . . although, with Smeeton, one was never sure there mightn't be a broken bottle or a bicycle chain. Not yet there hadn't, but Penn thought he might graduate before long. Penn dribbled a stone along the road, not altering course when a car hooted behind him. The road was a 'No Through Road' down to the river, and Penn reckoned he owned it. The car, a white Jaguar, edged him over, the driver glaring. Penn thumped its back wing for good measure and thought of some good adjectives for the driver.

'She went upstairs and the door he broke,
He found her hanging from a rope,' he sang.

Penn's voice was nothing special, but he knew verse after verse of the songs he sang, and the songs were neither in Mr Crocker's repertoire nor in the pop charts. It was Bates who had the voice. Bates who could sing: 'Oh, dig my grave long, wide, and deep', and wring your heart. Penn shot his stone straight and true into the flank of one of Mr Turner's heifers, regarding it through the barbed wire, and had the satisfaction of seeing it put up its tail and cavort away towards the sea-wall. Bates's father was Mr Turner's cowman. Bates had no trouble finding a holiday job; he just worked on the farm. Bates's father wouldn't have Penn. Penn didn't hold it against him.

He came down to Purvis's boatyard, climbed the sea-wall and surveyed the river, and the marshes beyond. His smack, or Smeeton's, was on a mooring in mid-stream, a sad, faded thing with swinging halyards. Purvis said it would fall to bits under them unless they did something to it, but they had no cash to spend on it, and nobody cared. It was rotten, but they only pottered on the river, when they could get its engine to go, or took it fishing up Fiddler's Creek. They had never taken it out to sea, save in calm weather. Penn had messed about on the river ever since he could remember. Old Purvis had taught him to sail years ago, and lent him a sailing dinghy which he had raced occasionally with Jim. He didn't rave about it, but it was quite a satisfactory way of passing time, and the old smack was a valuable hide-out. He and Bates used it quite often. They had a crate of beer in the forepeak, along with the fishing-lines. Penn looked at the old boat, *Mathilda*, with affection.

'You haven't been long,' Bates said, appearing at his elbow.

Penn grunted. They stood together, looking out over

the water. The sun was still well above the wall and it was warm enough to send the gnats spiralling. 'Warm enough to swim,' Penn said.

'Warm enough for *you*,' Bates qualified it. Bates couldn't swim, although he had played on the river all his life.

They fetched Jim's old dinghy and rowed out to *Mathilda*. It was Friday night, and some of the yachtsmen were down, fitting out. Purvis's yard boasted a line of yachts on moorings, very smart beside *Mathilda*. The man in the Jaguar was carrying an inflatable down the hard. Penn's eyes narrowed as he watched him.

'Think they own the place, some of these yachty blokes.'

Bates went below and stretched himself out on one of the bunks in the dark, cramped saloon. Penn followed him down, his bulk blotting out the light. Penn slouched along most of the time, looking shapeless and slack, but when he moved into action he was remarkably light on his feet. What looked like fat, when he was in his normal indolent posture, hands in pockets, shoulders rounded, was, in fact, all muscle. Beside him, Bates was a weedy specimen, a self-effacing, spotty-faced henchman. They were called Laurel and Hardy at school, out of Penn's hearing. Nobody knew what Penn saw in Bates.

Bates opened two cans of beer out of the cardboard box on the floor, and Penn hunched himself on the other bunk, elbows on knees, and started to play his harmonica.

'Keep an eye out for Smeeton,' he said, and played, very softly, 'Blowing in the Wind'.

'That old crap,' Bates groaned.

Penn knew that Bates needed the beer before he would mellow, the whole pint before he would sing, and two pints before he started singing well. Penn didn't mind the time lag, running through the tunes that came to mind, and trying out some train noises that might fit in with Bates's 'Freight Train'. All the songs Bates sang had to do with death. He only sang of executions, drownings, heartbreak, and suicide. The happier he got in his singing, the more melancholy were the things he sang about, so that when he sang 'Take me to the graveyard and lay the sod o'er me', Penn knew that he was really away. After that he would sing 'The Butcher Boy'.

'That sound like a train?'

'Ten-thirty out of Liverpool Street,' Bates said.

Penn, searching with his tongue for the American coyote call of the legendary prairie train, would have cursed him if he could. He snored into the harmonica, trying to find the right evocative rhythm, making it throb through the opening and closing of his hands.

'Sounds like the sea,' Bates said.

Penn listened to it, switching his mind from trains.

'Like under a groyne or something,' Bates said.

Penn tried it softer, lower down, less urgently. He saw what Bates meant.

'What could we use it for? Who gets drowned in your repertoire?'

Bates sat up suddenly. 'Smeeton,' he said.

Penn grinned. 'I wish he did.' He flung the harmonica down and looked out of the hatch.

'Yeah. Smeeton and Co. They've got Gerry's dinghy.'

Bates lay back on the bunk again. 'I'm not fighting,' he said.

Penn went up on deck. A low sun flooded the river with a golden evening light, and gilded the undersides of a drifting cumulus with a generosity that turned the prosaic river scene into a page out of a 'Beautiful Britain' calendar. In the cockpit of a shapely yawl on the next mooring, the London yachtsman, joined by a friend, admired the scene, a glass of gin in his hand, the red glow of a cigarette pricking his lips. Penn leaned against *Mathilda*'s shrouds, squinting into the brightness, working out a plan of campaign, his face eager and excited. Smeeton was rowing out from the hard, his friends trimming the small dinghy rather anxiously. The tide was running hard, and Smeeton was having difficulty keeping the dinghy up against it.

'I say, Bates! Come and watch this! What did you say about drowning Smeeton?'

Bates put his head out and found Penn stripping off his clothes, capering about on one foot with the other stuck in his jeans.

'I didn't say anything,' Bates said.

'I'm going to sink him.'

Bates smiled. 'Watch he doesn't lay you under with an oar.' He folded his arms on the hatch, impressed with Penn's idea.

'I don't want to get mashed,' Penn said. 'I can't hold off four.'

Stripped down to resplendent red underpants, he cupped his hands to his mouth and bellowed, 'Smeeton, you basket! Start praying *now*!'

Bates laughed. Penn did a racing dive off the stern of the smack and struck out for the plodding dinghy with his powerful splashy stroke. Bates, coming up on deck to get a good view, sensed immediate paralysis strike the dinghy as the significance of Penn's move sunk in. Smeeton stopped rowing, drawing in his oars, and the dinghy started to move off sideways on the tide. It was well out from the bank and Penn was moving too fast to make retreat a likely possibility, but Smeeton, recovering from his first shock, had the sense to start rowing again with the tide, straight down the river, to make as much speed as possible. Penn, seeing his manoeuvre, quickened his pace, and started to overhaul the dinghy.

Smeeton stopped rowing.

'Stow it, Pennington, you lousy creep!'

'Warm as toast!' Penn shouted. 'You'll love it!'

Smeeton pulled in one oar and lifted the other out of its rowlock. He had to move very carefully, for there was only about six inches of freeboard on the dinghy. His friends, two in the stern and one in the bows, sat tensely, muttering advice. The dinghy was now opposite the yawl, *Escape*, and the two men in the cockpit were watching the drama as closely as Bates.

Penn knew that Smeeton was a sitting duck. He flung back his hair and laughed. He swam in close, watching Smeeton carefully. Smeeton lifted up his oar, but Penn, fractionally out of range, rolled under the water and disappeared.

'Sit still!' Smeeton hissed. He waved the oar, narrowly missing the head of the boy in the stern who was watching the trail of bubbles that ran on the tide. The dinghy drifted, serene as a swan, crab-wise on the water. All four boys gripped the gunwales, eyes flicking the water.

'*Yaaaaah!*' Penn surfaced so close and with such energy that Smeeton thought he had come on board. He was the opposite side from where they had all been expecting him. Everyone in the dinghy swung round. Smeeton lashed out with his oar, dropped it in his eagerness and lunged forward to retrieve it. The dinghy dropped one corner of its transom under, and immediately the water poured in all over one side. Smeeton stood and leapt, instantly, straight for Pennington's grinning face. They submerged together, Smeeton's epithets dissolved in another flurry of bubbles. Penn, the water roaring in his ears, was enjoying himself. He knew Smeeton did not fight fair, and was not prepared to give him a chance, either under water or on top. When he eventually came up for breath, he had his hand firmly on Smeeton's face, holding it under.

'I say!' The shout, in cultured accents, rasped across the water. 'I say, you boys!'

The two yachtsmen had launched their rubber dinghy and were rowing out. Penn, feeling Smeeton failing beneath him, took his hand off his face and pulled him up by his hair.

'You lousy – stinking—' Smeeton was almost sobbing with rage.

'Leave that poor boy alone, you young hooligan!'

Penn, submerging Smeeton once more, looked up into the face of *Escape*'s skipper. He saw a little military moustache fairly bristling with military rage, outraged eyes like glass chips.

'You young thug! I'll get the police to you!'

Penn swum free of Smeeton, leaving him to his own devices, and turned and faced the yachtsmen in their smart white caps. He flung his hair back, deliberately, so that it sent a shower of water across the frosty expressions. He then started to swim towards them, submerging after two strokes. The glass chips glazed momentarily.

Penn swam underneath the rubber dinghy, his back rubbing the bulges that were the two yachtsmen's seats. He rolled over and rocked the dinghy, quite gently, feeling its smooth surface against him like some friendly whale. He felt the bulges betray alarm in a most satisfactory manner. He laughed, belching up a roaring froth of air. He rocked the dinghy until his breath ran out, then he kicked away and swam out, making for *Mathilda* without looking back.

The new constable rode down to Purvis's yard at dusk, conscientiously familiarizing himself with his area. He was very keen, and liked to think he was working hard, but in fact it was pleasant enough, chatting up the locals, seeing the caution in their eyes. A big Jaguar was parked on the edge of the lane, which he noted. He got off his bike and pushed it up the gravel incline to the top of the sea-wall, where he stood silhouetted, an unmistakable figure of authority.

Purvis, locking up his shed for the night, said to Jim, 'Here's trouble.'

He shifted the cap on his forehead, and put the key in his pocket.

'Evening, constable,' he said.

'Lovely spot,' said the constable matily.

'So they say.'

'I'm new to this area. Mitchell's my name. Just having a look round, getting to know what's where, so to speak.'

'You're instead of PC Perkins, then? Helping Sergeant West, like?'

'That's right.'

'I'm Purvis. Run the yard here. This is my son, Jim.'

They stood in a row, looking out over the darkening water. The wind was light and the water was quiet, near the end of the ebb, so that banks of glistening mud lay uncovered, plopping and trickling here and there, the occasional curlew twittering uneasily. From the big white yawl lights glowed through the ports, very cosy. The glow from *Mathilda* was subdued by comparison, a faint flush in the open hatchway. But a sound came with it, very plaintive and soft on the damp spring air, a voice singing, accompanied by a reedy descant on the harmonica, full of sorrow and longing. The three men could not help but listen, the lament coming and going with the breathing of the wind, laced with the curlew's flitterings, and the water running through the outfalls from Mr Turner's pasture. The last note was held, very pure and free, clearly carried by the wind. There was a silence of a few seconds, then a raucous laugh and the sound of an empty tin being flung overboard, some thumping and cursing, and a few bars of 'Nellie Dean', sung very coarsely.

Jim Purvis cleared his throat. 'You coming, Dad?'

'Aye.'

'You lose any gear, a place like this . . . valuable stuff lying around?' the constable asked.

'We've lost a couple of echo-sounders, the odd pair of oars and suchlike. Nothing big, as yet.'

Jim fidgeted with the money in his pocket. There was a silence again, and into it the sound of oars plugging into the ebb. The constable peered down the causeway.

'That'll be Major Harmsworth, off the yawl,' Purvis told him. 'He'll be going up to the Crown for the evening.'

'That his Jag?'

'That's right. He's from London.'

They waited until the Major and his friend came up the hard. The Major had a reefer jacket and gum boots with white edges.

'Evening, Purvis,' he said.

'Evening, sir.'

The Major looked at the constable and said, 'You should have been here a bit earlier. Who's the lout on the smack, Purvis – got hair like a girl?'

'That'll be young Pennington, sir. Lives in the village.'

'He's a danger to the community, the way he carries on. Ought to be locked up. He sank a dinghy with four young lads aboard, just now. Might have drowned the lot of them. He damned nearly sank us, too.'

Jim grinned, turning away, but old Purvis said, 'Really, sir?' his expression not changing.

'You heard of him?' the Major asked the constable.

'I'm brand-new around here, sir. Just been telling Mr Purvis here, I'm making acquaintance of my area.'

'Well, you keep an eye on him. It'll pay you.'

'Sergeant West knows all about him,' Purvis said.

'He's got a record, no doubt?' barked the Major.

Purvis did not reply. 'You locked the other shed?' he asked Jim. Jim nodded. 'We'll be getting along now, then. Good night, sir. Good night, Mr Mitchell.'

They all went their separate ways, by bicycle and by Jaguar. The river settled into silence again, until the tide turned, and the boats on the moorings started to swing, snubbing gently on their chains. The harmonica wailed, its natural stridency gentled by pure skill into a strange, plaintive beauty. With it Bates's voice came once more, its hesitancy forgotten, mellifluous with beer and confidence, spilling into the night.

Long after Major Harmsworth and his friend had returned to their boat and gone to sleep, Penn and Bates rowed ashore and pulled Jim's boat up above the watermark. They moved rather unsteadily, and laughed a good deal, lapsing into, 'I say, I say, boy! Look what you're doing!' at every blunder. Bates stood on top of the sea-wall, swaying slightly.

'What you going to do when you leave, Penn?' he said.

'Leave where?'

'School, you fool.'

'I'm going to enjoy myself.'

'No. Really.'

'Oh, don't make me miserable! What a subject!'

'I want to sing,' said Bates, earnestly. 'Sing properly, on the telly.'

'It'll cost you a fortune in beer,' Penn said. He was standing beside Bates, contemplating the gleaming Jaguar below him.

'I mean it, though.'

'You! You don't open your beak except on the boat where you think no one can hear you! Why didn't you sing in the school concert when you were asked? You, on the telly—' His voice grated with scorn.

Bates was silent.

'I'll tell you what,' Penn said. He slithered down the wall on to the grass and stood beside the Jaguar. 'What I feel like, I mean. What would give me the greatest pleasure in the whole wide world—'

'What, Penn?'

Bates staggered down the wall. He saw Penn stoop down beside the Jaguar's back wheel, and heard the explosive hiss of air escaping from the valve. The Jaguar sank gradually to an askew angle, looking rather quaint. Penn went round and treated the opposite wheel in the same fashion and then to the front. The Jaguar squatted, pathetic in the thin starlight.

Bates giggled.

'I say, I say, boy, you shouldn't have done that!' He kept repeating it all the way home.

CHAPTER TWO

'PAT! FOR HEAVEN'S sake!'

Penn was awoken by his mother shaking him violently by the shoulder.

'What you been up to? Jim Purvis is at the door, and says his father wants to see you, no messing. He's raving, he says.'

'Let him rave,' Penn grunted.

'Get out, you lazy oaf. It's gone eight.' She threw back the blankets and stared in exasperation at the great bare shoulders hunched against her. 'God, Pat, your hair! When you going to the barber's, for heaven's sake? Get out now, and come down and see what Jim wants. It's no joke from the look of him.'

'Oh, lay off!' Penn muttered.

'Come on! I know trouble when I see it. You won't get a second chance. I've told you before. You put a finger wrong again and they'll have you in one of those places where you do everything at the double. And good luck to you, I say. You won't be able to lie in bed—'

'For cripes' sake!' Penn surfaced into reality, baited into consciousness. He heaved himself from the bed, thudding on to the floor. 'Stop laying into me, this time o' the morning! I've got to sleep, haven't I? A growing boy – we get it at school. They *tell* us we've got to get eight hours, and here's you—'

'Growing! You grow any more and you can go into a circus for a freak! Pity your brain isn't a match for your brawn! If I hadn't had my own way you'd have been out of that school on your ear by now, and working for your living! You've got me to thank—'

'Thank!' Penn sat on the side of the bed, feeling himself shake with desolation and nausea. 'Cripes, I've got nothing to thank you for! If I was working for a living I could leave home – I might get some peace.'

'That's a fine way to show your gratitude!'

'Gratitude! For God's sake, you only had me because you weren't blooming clever enough – what have I got to be grateful for?'

Penn swore at his mother. When she started laying into him he felt he would like to strangle her. When she was in one of her raves, which was often.

'Get out!' he said. 'I want to get dressed. I thought you wanted me to hurry or something.'

The door slammed. Penn groaned. He started to dress, trying to dredge up out of the blankness in his head the thing that was making Purvis rage. He remembered Smeeton. He wasn't in trouble over that, surely? He thudded downstairs, combing his hair as he went.

'What's up, Jim?'

Jim was in the kitchen, looking agitated, for him. Jim was a slow-moving, imperturbable young man of few words, but today he was crisp.

'You'd better come, Pat. It's no good thinking you can get away with it. Dad sent me to fetch you.'

Penn shrugged.

'I'll just have my breakfast and—'

'He said at once.'

Penn shrugged again. His father wasn't home yet, luckily. He got his jacket and fetched his bicycle out of the shed. Old Purvis's rage seemed to have rubbed off on Jim, for Jim was cold and short. They cycled down the lane in silence, while Penn searched back in his mind to the evening before. Apart from the highly satisfying Smeeton episode, one other thing had given him great comfort. For some minutes he couldn't remember what it was. Then when they came to the part of the lane where the car had overtaken him the day before, he said to Jim, 'It's not to do with that Jag, is it?'

'Oh, Pat, you're a ruddy fool,' Jim said. 'I tried to stick up for you, but—' He sighed.

They came down to the yard, Penn not caring terribly. It was only the valves, after all. Jim was acting as if he'd carved the tyres with a knife. It was only a bit of fun.

Old Purvis was standing beside the flattened Jaguar. Penn rode up to him, not very enthusiastically, and as he came alongside the car the reason for the peculiar Purvis emotion was made plain. Painted with tar in crude black letters all along the car's side was an unmentionable four-letter word.

Penn's face went tight, in a way Soggy would have recognized. Smeeton's crafty face swam before his vision and was mangled out of recognition by all the things Penn wished on it. One look at Purvis's expression, and Penn felt the injustices of the whole wide world belting him in the empty stomach regions; all the cries that welled through his indignation were those of a child: 'It's not fair! I didn't do it!' But he said nothing. The shock, with its wild emotions, flared and died. It was almost, for a moment, as if – because they all expected these things of him – he could easily have done it, almost wished he had. The situation was not new to Penn.

'Well?' Purvis barked.

'I didn't do it,' Penn said.

'You're standing there, large as life, and telling me you never touched this car?'

K. M. Peyton

'Yes, I ruddy well am,' Penn said.

'You said, up the lane, was it to do with the Jag?' Jim put in stolidly.

'Yes, it was the tyres I meant.'

'You let the tyres down?' Purvis said.

'Yes, I let the tyres down, but I didn't write that stuff. You won't believe me, will you? Well, I'm not wasting my breath saying anything else.'

'No, you can use it on the Major when he comes ashore,' Purvis said shortly. 'And if you didn't do it, you're going to carry the can for whoever did, my boy. You lads are all as bad as one another round here. I let you keep that wreck on a mooring out there, and all I get from you is trouble. You start bothering my customers and that's my livelihood. So I'm telling you, I've had enough. You can explain to the Major when he comes ashore, and while you're waiting you can start trying to clean it up. We've got a foot-pump you can start on the tyres with. I doubt you'll get the tar off, but you can try. I reckon it'll need a respray when it's off, and the bill will go to your father. Now get moving!'

Penn, seeing when he was beaten, got moving. He pumped the tyres up, which, with Purvis's inadequate pump, took a long time. Far longer than it had taken to let them down.

'Lucky you're fit,' Jim said.

30

Penn scowled. 'I'm not doing anything to the message, seeing as I didn't write it.'

Jim said, 'I would. Dad was all for getting the police in, but I managed to cool him down. If you play him up now, he'll tell West what's happened.'

Choked by the injustice, Penn looked down at the sticky can of dissolvent Jim produced. He was ravenously hungry. Jim brought him a cup of tea at eleven and squatted down beside him, surveying Penn's work.

'It's taking the ruddy cellulose off as well,' Penn said. 'It's going to need a respray.'

'Just as well the Major's gone sailing. He should be in a good mood when he gets back.'

'Not for long he won't be,' Penn commented. He was fed up with the amusement of the visitors to the boatyard, seeing what had happened to the Major's Jaguar. Saturday morning was busy. He had received plenty of advice, all of it facetious. He felt like writing the same message six foot high all along the side of Purvis's shed. When he had finished at one o'clock the message could be read, not in tar, but in the matt trail worked by the dissolvent over the otherwise glossy surface.

'It *is* going to need a respray.' Jim's statement of the obvious did nothing to improve Penn's spirits. He could not bring himself to say anything. He viciously booted the can he had been using into Purvis's tip and turned away to get his bike. The job his father had been urging him to get for the holidays seemed suddenly very desirable. Something, he thought, where he wouldn't have people on his back all the time, niggling, nagging . . . 'Get your hair cut' . . . 'Take your hands out of your pockets' . . . The teachers at school – with two possible exceptions, to be fair – were all counting the hours till he left. Several of them, under provocation, had told him so. But no employers were lining up for his services either. His mother was pleased when he went out and disapproving when he came in. Penn rarely thought of all these underlying grievances, but the thought of his father being presented with a bill for the Jaguar's respray was prompting an instinctive scrub round for a line of defence. Not that his father was going to hear anything about the story from him . . .

'What was it all about, then?' his mother asked him. 'Your dinner's half cold. I turned the oven out an hour ago.'

'Oh, nothing.'

'You going out this afternoon?'

'Yeah.' He would make sure he was out around the time Major Harmsworth was likely to return from his sail.

'If you go down Moorham you can get your hair cut.'

Penn did not reply.

He went upstairs and washed and shaved and put a clean shirt on and went to call on Bates. Bates was watching soccer on the television, but came out when he saw that Penn had something to tell him.

'I'll get my bike.'

Picking morosely at the privet hedge, Penn told the tale of the Jaguar while Bates disentangled his bike from a clutter of gardening tools and gum boots. Bates was duly appalled.

'What'll your father do when he gets that bill, then?'

Penn shrugged.

'No one'll believe I didn't do it, not after I was fool enough to say I did the tyres. They all know we were down there till gone midnight. Smeeton knew what he was doing all right. I'll corpse him next time I lay eyes on him.'

They cycled abreast down the lane signposted to Moorham, scowling into the grey, damp afternoon. Moorham, a mile down the river from Fiddler's End, the village they lived in, was a small unlively town, given over to a desultory boat-building industry. It was three miles from the sea, and boasted one or two fishing-boats which unloaded occasionally at the jetty, several rows of yachts and motor launches on moorings, and a flotsam of small craft of all shapes and sizes pulled up on the mud or out on the wall. Apart from the boat-building there was no industry, other than the few cafés that fed the weekend influx. The children that passed out from the local primary school went, along with the Fiddler's End children, to the Beehive Secondary Modern in the nearest big town, twelve miles away by school bus. Penn and Bates went to Moorham at weekends to get a Coke and ten cigarettes, and eye the birds that walked along the quay; perhaps, if they were lucky, take over the ferryman's job for an hour while he went for a drink (because George knew that whatever else Penn's failings, the boy knew how to use a boat in the strong tide and could bring the launch into the quay without smashing anything). Apart from that, there was the odd scuffle with the local opposition, a scrounge down on the shore to see if there was anything to pick up, or a barracking of the local soccer talent on the playing-field, all of which passed the time, if nothing else.

They went into the café on the quay and sat staring out of the steamy windows. Bates offered Penn a cigarette, but said nothing, recognizing the heavy despair in Penn's face. Even when cheerful, Penn's face had an aggressive cast. Scowling, the heavy jaw pushed forward, lower lip thrusting, small blue-grey eyes bitterly reflective, his looks cast him to perfection into the role of thug, a word he heard too often. He had no illusions as to his looks, but was proud of his physique, which he perversely disguised by his slouching posture. He was also proud of his hair, and it pleased him that its length annoyed his parents, and was beginning to worry Soggy. Nobody at school had got away with hair as long as his, yet. The future in this direction promised interest. Meanwhile, the immediate future promised only trouble of a less subtle nature.

'There's Dotty,' Bates said, scrubbing a hole in the steam on the windows.

Dotty was often to be seen in Moorham, for he was a devout fisherman. He went out to sea in a tiny outboard dinghy, and sat anchored for hours off the sand banks watching his line. Music and fishing were the only interests in his life, each as holy as the other. Penn sensed that Dotty, out fishing, recharged his batteries during long hours of solitude so that he was capable of coping with life at the Beehive. A gentle man by nature, Dotty was forced to act in his job with a severity that came to him uneasily, not instinctively – as it did to Soggy and a few more Penn could quickly name. This mixture of nature and assumption caused Dotty to act eccentrically, getting carried away equally by the beauty of music and the unbeauty of the Beehive boys, so that he steered an erratic course through lessons between tender, all-loving enthusiasm and demoniacal fury. Penn was quite fond of him, in an unthinking way. He also liked the games master, a young, bullet-headed man called Matthews. All the other teachers he either despised or loathed with a completeness equalled only by their similar feelings towards him.

'Nut-case,' Bates muttered, watching Dotty crouching over his outboard, trying to get it to start. The tide was out, and was already carrying Dotty's boat down towards a line of moored yachts. The boys knew that when he hit one Dotty would raise his cap to the owner if he happened to be on board and say, 'I beg your pardon.' Dotty was well known in Moorham.

Penn, his glance bored with Dotty, brought it idly back to the quayside. Bates saw him stiffen.

'Oh, Bates!' he whispered. He stubbed his cigarette out in the ashtray and stood up.

Bates looked through the hole in the steam and saw Smeeton coming along the quay with Gerry and Gary Green, and a red-haired, very thin boy called Fletcher. His eyes swivelled quickly up to Penn's.

'You ought to be careful, Penn.'

It was a bit different, he was thinking, attacking in the centre of Moorham on a Saturday afternoon, compared with out on the deserted shore at Fiddler's

End. But Penn was already away. Bates finished his Coke, and followed him reluctantly.

Penn waited in the doorway of the café until Smeeton, unaware, came abreast of him. The quayside was about twenty feet wide, and on the far side there was a wall, and a drop down to the low-tide mud some twelve feet below. Opposite the café the wall gave on to the wooden jetty where the fishing-boats unloaded. Penn stepped out, leading with his shoulder in such a way that Smeeton was pushed right across the quay and on to the jetty before he knew what had hit him. Penn knew he could only put Smeeton where he wanted him by working fast. Fletcher and the Green brothers were no mean fighters, not pacifists like Bates.

Smeeton went sprawling, shouting with pure funk. Penn stooped down and dragged him bodily to the edge of the jetty by one leg, and got him half over the edge before Smeeton's reinforcements moved in. Penn braced himself, stamped hard on Smeeton's clutching fingers, and had the satisfaction of seeing him go before Gary Green's head hit him in the diaphragm. Penn's diaphragm was up to plenty of weight. Penn swung round and barged Green while he was still in momentum from his own attack, and Green sailed over the end of the jetty like a diver at high water. Penn had a momentary regret that Smeeton hadn't gone with the same velocity, but then recognized immediately that he was going to be hard put to stay on top himself. Fletcher brought him down while he was still off balance, and they rolled viciously together, over and over, across the width of the jetty. Fletcher was inspired by the dangerous knowledge that he might have bitten off more than he could chew, and was glad to see Gerry Green hovering, waiting to bring his boot into the right man's ribs.

Penn was strong and furious enough to be almost a match for the two boys together, and the three bodies, flailing across the wooden jetty, proved an irresistible attraction to what seemed to Bates a very fair proportion of the population of Moorham. Bates stood, like a referee, watching Penn, and sizing up the gathering crowd. He was anxious, but not alarmed, experienced in supervising Penn in similar situations, aware that an incensed old lady brandishing an umbrella was about to inflict on him a good deal more punishment than either Fletcher or Green was so far managing.

'You wicked boys! You ought to be ashamed of yourselves!' The umbrella caught Penn smartly across the ear, so that he looked up in surprise and saw, for the first time, the size of his audience. His moment's inattention gave Fletcher the opportunity to roll clear.

Like a flash he turned and dropped a knee across Penn's throat, and Gerry, for the first time, got a clear aim for his boot. He swung in with a grunt of satisfaction, but Penn got an arm up in time and jerked him off balance while the kick was still in mid-air. Green fell heavily, and Penn crashed a fist into his ear which made him shout. Fletcher, shaken off momentarily, came back with a blow that Penn was too late to duck. It made him shake his head and swear furiously, but Fletcher found himself immediately on the ground again, Penn's great hand round his neck. He thrashed out wildly, and the two of them rolled dangerously to the edge of the jetty.

Bates frowned. He could not see Penn getting free of both boys in a hurry, and the crowd was now getting agitated. Some women with shopping baskets were urging the nearest male spectators to do something.

'It's downright disgraceful, right in the middle of the town! Can't you stop them?'

The young men grinned, enjoying themselves, but an older, respectable-looking man and the proprietor of the café pushed their way to the front and advanced gingerly.

'I've rung the police,' the café proprietor said.

'Ruddy young hooligans,' the other man said.

'I saw who started it.'

While they were talking the old lady moved in and

speared Penn in the ribs with such force that he let out a yell. He flung Fletcher away from him and rolled up on his knees. Bates got in beside him and said urgently, 'Pack it in, Penn! The coppers are coming!' The lady with the umbrella then hit Bates so hard across the face that he went sprawling half over the side of the jetty.

The crowd let out a cheer. 'Go for it, old girl!'

Penn grabbed Bates and heaved him up by one arm, felt someone come up close behind him and instinctively swung round, fist raised, aware of his precarious position. The fist was already moving when Penn became conscious of the fact that his new assailant was neither Fletcher nor Green. His reaction was instant, the force behind the blow snatched away in mid-air, but the falling knuckles brushed flesh.

'Like that, is it?' said the police constable.

'Oh, cripes,' said Penn very quietly. He stood still, hands hanging, and tossed back his hair. Bates stood close behind him, refereeing still, but seeing only total defeat.

'What's all this about, then? Who started it?'

The police constable was brisk and very young. Penn was puzzled by not knowing him, realizing he must be new. Mitchell put out a hand, closing it round Penn's upper arm.

'He started it,' said the man from the café, gesturing

at Penn. 'He set on two young fellows and threw them off the end of the jetty.'

'That right?' said Mitchell to Penn.

'Yes, but—'

'The buts can wait. What's your name?'

'Pennington.'

'Oh, is it?' Mitchell looked pleased, and Penn guessed that he knew all about him, new as he was. He glanced over the jetty and said, 'These the boys you attacked?'

Penn looked round and saw Smeeton and Gary Green coming up the jetty steps. For a short, lovely moment he was happy. They were both plastered in liquid mud from head to foot. They came up to Mitchell, and Penn grinned and said to Smeeton, 'It's good for pimples. I was just doing you a favour.'

'I'll do you a favour. I'll come and visit you in Oakhall,' Smeeton said. Oakhall was a detention centre.

Mitchell started sorting things out. If it had been West, Penn thought, he would have stood a chance, but this new man was too keen. Several of the crowd were only too anxious to tell him what had happened, and the café proprietor's evidence was damning.

'I saw this boy attack the others as they were walking past. They gave him no provocation at all. He just went straight for them . . .'

Mitchell diligently took the man's name and address. Penn stood scowling, waiting. One of the women said, 'What he wants is a good hiding. A dose of the birch. It should never have been done away with.'

'Nor hanging either!'

'Too soft with 'em these days . . .'

'Never did a bully any harm, that sort of treatment.'

'Just gave him a stiff neck,' Bates muttered.

'I'll give you all the evidence you want,' said the café man to Mitchell. 'I'm tired of these yobbos. Be glad to see them get their deserts.'

Mitchell turned back to Penn.

'I'm arresting you for assault . . .'

Penn wasn't surprised. The tension went out of him, and he slumped, frowning and silent.

'You'd better come along to the station. You others can beat it.'

Penn knew his own way to the station, and headed through the crowd, glowering, his hands in his pockets. He was on his own now, and the spindly, anxious figure of the disappearing Bates wrenched him with self-pity. He thought fleetingly of his mother and father and then, not fleetingly at all, of Oakhall. The familiar polish and disinfectant smell of the police station closed round him.

'All right,' said Mitchell. 'Turn round. Face the wall. Put your hands up.'

Mitchell went through all Penn's pockets, dropping everything he found on the floor. Penn leaned his hands against the wall, very careful not to say anything, feeling all the excesses of hatred flushing through his body, almost surprised that Mitchell was not receiving live shocks of it through his filthy inquisitive fingers. The search finished, Penn did not move. He knew all about martinets like Mitchell.

Mitchell went to a file, rifled through, and started reading. The telephone rang and he answered it, and took down a long list of particulars about a lost dog, then went back to the file again. When he had finished he said, 'Pick up your things.'

Penn was picking them up when Sergeant West came in. West looked thoughtfully at Penn.

'What are you doing here?'

'Ask him,' Penn said bitterly, with a jerk of his head in Mitchell's direction.

'I've arrested him for assault,' Mitchell said coldly.

He explained the circumstances and West listened, watching Penn with his disappointed-father look, which Penn did not like.

'Why did you go for Smeeton?' West asked.

'Because he got me into trouble down at Purvis's — something he did and I got the blame for, and no one will believe I didn't do it—'

'To do with a Jaguar?'

'Yes.'

'Hm.'

Penn waited. West knew about the Jaguar; there were no secrets, as if the very seagulls scattered the scandal about the marshes, screaming it from raucous, jeering bills. No doubt Fiddler's End was already receiving intimations of the latest dust-up in Moorham.

West said to Mitchell, 'Put him in the detention room for ten minutes.'

Mitchell opened the door for him. Penn slouched through, heard the key turn in the lock behind him. The room was small, furnished merely with filing cabinets, a table, two chairs, and an ashtray. Penn walked round it twice, and found that all the filing cabinets were locked, then he sat down on one of the chairs. He knew it would be Oakhall for him this time. Oakhall and all the stories he had heard about it preoccupied him; the old, familiar, scorned threat used by both his parents and, on occasion, by Soggy and Stacker, came very close and sharp, and all his thick, pent-up truculence gave way to what felt ominously like a case of the panics. He got out a cigarette, his fingers jerky, then remembered that it was Bates who had the matches. He put his arms down on the table and rested his head on his wrist and said, 'Oh cripes! Oh God, I don't want to go there!'

After a few minutes he became aware of a sharp, unpleasant pain in his side which puzzled him, until he remembered the old girl with the umbrella. He pulled up his shirt and found an impressive red abrasion, flecked with blood.

'The old buzzard! If Mitchell's going to charge me with assault, he's got nothing to show for it. I could charge her with assault, a thing like this!'

He remembered Smeeton and the mud, and smiled, then he remembered the Jaguar and old Purvis's face, and Oakhall, and he got up and walked round the room, kicking at the filing cabinets. Outside he heard the boys going home from the playing-field, still punting the ball with hollow thuds across the road, and the sudden smell of soccer, the crushed grass and the sour leather, the sweat and salt of it on the tongue, made him suddenly feel as if he had been at it himself, out in the road. It gave him a twist of feeling that he could put no name to; it was like a pain, a great longing for something without identity; it made him feel sick for being where he was, and the thought of Oakhall. He didn't think his home was anything much, but, by God, he didn't want to be taken away and pushed around by blokes like Mitchell. It was quite silent after the boys had gone, as if the whole of Moorham had gone home to tea. He sat, and the smell of polish and the dumb evidence of the filing cabinets, full of records of petty crime, hung in the room, a dusty smog of wretchedness.

It was a very long ten minutes.

When eventually the door opened and West came in he got nervously to his feet, but West beckoned him to sit down again. Penn slumped back, and West sat on the edge of the desk.

'You're a darned young fool, Patrick. It's high time you grew up, time you learned to think. You don't *think*, do you, Pat?'

There was no answer to that. No help to say what he thought about coppers like Mitchell. He had thoughts all right. He sat scowling, feeling himself going down. West was watching him, lips pursed.

'You leaving school in July?'

'Yes, sir.'

'Thought what you're going to do?'

'I've *thought*, but—' Penn shrugged. Back to thoughts again. It hadn't got him far.

'Anything you do at school give you an interest? You get any sort of training for a trade?'

'All we get is useless, sir. History and geography and reading old plays and things, and a load about God. Doesn't get you a job.'

'Woodwork? Metalwork? Nothing like that?'

'I made a coffee-table . . .' Penn frowned. His

mother had put a trayload of cups and saucers on it and it had collapsed and two cups were broken. She had sent a letter of complaint to the woodwork master, who had given Penn a detention for shoddy work. Penn wasn't allowed in the metalwork room; the master said the equipment was too valuable to let Pennington loose on it.

'I can't even get a job for the holidays,' he said, to avoid the question. 'That's what I came to Moorham for this afternoon, to see if I could find a job.'

'You hardly went the right way about it,' West said drily.

'No, sir.'

'You've got yourself a bad reputation, Pennington. You can't afford a bad reputation in a small place like this. You're not stupid. You've done badly at school, workwise, because you're lazy and undisciplined, not because you're stupid. You go on acting this way and you'll find yourself in bad trouble once you start trying to earn money. You know all this, don't you?'

'Yes, sir.'

'Well, look, I'm not accepting Mitchell's charge. I know you young kids like a fight, and there's no harm in it, only *you*, of course, have to be fool enough to start it right in the middle of town. Bit daft, wasn't it? Try to use your loaf, Pennington, that's all I ask. I don't want to see you in here again – please bear it in mind.'

Penn felt himself coming up, shining and cheering, out of the deep water. The little bare room danced round him. He had a sense of freedom, of all the river and the shore and the sea and the fields lying there unchanged, and the steamy cafés to comfort, even the old Beehive familiar about him, a womb of lesser evil than the dreaded Oakhall.

West saw him to the door. Mitchell watched him, and Penn could tell that he was furious. He was another enemy now, as good as Smeeton. Penn revelled in the thought, seeing the grey evening through the door, the puddles shining in the street.

'Goodbye, Pennington. Don't come back.'

'No, sir. Thank you, sir.'

Penn ran down the street, the release of energy bursting in his heels. He went across the quay and skimmed a few stones across the water, shook back his hair and looked up at the grey wet sky. If he was Bates, he would be singing, 'Take me to the graveyard . . .' 'Oh, Bates boy! We're all right!' Penn sang, and scuffled a stone down the quay. He would fetch his bike, and go and knock up Bates. 'Cripes, I'm ravenous! Not even a cup of mouldy prison tea! That new copper's as mean as a snake.' He went past the jetty and the café to the wall where he had left his bike. It wasn't there.

He looked at the blank wall, swelling with indignation.

'Some lousy creep's knocked it off!' It was a good bike. His father had got it cheap because it had already, earlier in its history, been knocked off. Penn had not thought it would happen to the same bike twice.

The wall belonged to a pub, the Green Man, which looked out over the river. As Penn stood there, kicking the wall, wondering if Bates had put it somewhere, a man came out of the side door of the pub and said, 'If you're looking for a bike, it's in my back yard.' He pushed a gate open and jerked his head to indicate that Penn could go inside. Penn nodded. The back windows of the pub showed the glow of light through from the bar. Penn could hear the Saturday night voices, careless and cheerful, and smell the meat pies in the oven through the open kitchen door. The landlord's wife put her head out, saw her husband and said in a harassed voice, 'For heaven's sake, Arthur, get a move on! I'm run off my feet. There's a sinkful of glasses to wash. I can't do everything. What a night for Joe to pack it in!'

Penn turned to Arthur and said, 'I'll help you out.'

'Get in there, then,' Arthur said.

Penn had got himself a job.

CHAPTER THREE

WHEN HE WAS washing up, Penn realized that he had only taken on the job because he was afraid to go home. His parents would know all about the incident on the quay by now: he had just had evidence of how fast news travelled in this area. He cursed himself for a fool, groping for a slice of lemon that was blocking up the plug. Washing up for a job! He must have been demented.

'How old are you?' the nagging woman asked him belligerently.

'Sixteen.'

'Don't set a foot out of this kitchen, then, or we'll have trouble. I'll bring the glasses out here, and you can see to the pies. And that sliced loaf, get it buttered. Here's the butter. Look sharp.'

She was worse than his mother.

But at eleven when the pub shut, Arthur gave him twelve and sixpence and said, 'If you're at a loose end the next fortnight, d'you fancy a job? The wife's going away and I can't do the cleaning. Can't get down on the floor, like. If you could come in, say, seven in the morning, till opening time. How old are you?'

'Sixteen.'

'Oh, I thought you was older. You look eighteen to me. Pity. I could use you in the bar if you were eighteen, while the wife's away. But if you're sixteen—' He shrugged.

Penn considered. He knew the chicken factory wouldn't take him unless he got his hair cut. Unhygienic, the foreman said. The only other alternative was to go to his father's place, labouring. Even scrubbing the pub floor would be better than his father's company all day, especially after the bill for the Jaguar put in its appearance.

'I could still clean up, couldn't I? Out of hours – it'd be all right, wouldn't it?'

'If you want to do it, yes.'

Arthur was obviously a man who took an easy course in life. 'Yes, you come in if you fancy it. I might find you something to do outside, too. That yard needs tidying up. I've been saying it for the last ten years.'

Penn had noticed. He had got himself employed, for better or for worse. And as it turned out, it was a very satisfactory arrangement, for Arthur was easy; he did not nag or scold or disapprove. Arthur suffered himself, from his wife, and when his wife was away he liked Penn, who said very little. Penn cleaned up early, and when the pub opened he went and worked in the yard, cleaning out the piles of lumber and junk in the sheds, the accumulation of decades, burning all the rubbish. He worked slowly, to spin the job out for the whole holiday, but Arthur did not mind. The bill for the Jaguar came for Mr Pennington (for the sum of ninety-six pounds eleven shillings). Penn's father gave him a pasting and threw it on the fire, and Penn took to using *Mathilda* as his pad, to keep out of the way of his father.

One lunch-time, when Penn was tending his bonfire, Mitchell saw him when he came out of the pub to use the gents. Mitchell was off duty, but he stared at Penn and said, 'What are you doing here?'

'Working.'

Penn reckoned Mitchell was, too, by the way his eyes took everything in. When the pub was shut at two-thirty Penn went into the kitchen, where Arthur had a meat pie and a pot of tea waiting.

Arthur said, 'Why's that copper interested in you? Asking me all about you, he was.'

Penn told him.

'He's too keen,' Arthur said. 'You don't want that in a little place like this. Just makes trouble.'

Penn agreed. 'He wants me shut up.'

'You be careful,' said Arthur.

It started to lash down with rain outside. Arthur settled down to watch horse-racing on the television, and Penn went to sweep out the bar. He leaned on his broom by the glass door of the public bar, scowling at the squally water beyond the quay. He hadn't anywhere to go, or anyone to see, and there was nothing to go home for, save nagging. Looking at the rain, he could think of nothing – not one thing in the whole wide world – that gave him one moment's stir of anticipatory pleasure. (Apart, of course, from the purely hallucinatory dreams of mashing Soggy and Mitchell and Smeeton and Stacker and setting fire to the Beehive, and the shadow of Oakhall, and Mitchell's pants, and the white Jaguar . . .). Even soccer, the best way of passing time, was packed in for this gloomy, puking, compulsory period of forced labour known as the summer term that hovered on the immediate horizon. If I grow my hair long enough, I'll get suspended, Penn thought, and at once, he felt better.

There was an old piano in the corner of the bar, and he opened it and tried a few chords to see if it worked. It did, and was in tune. He could hear Arthur snoring in the back, and the commentary jerking spasmodically from fence to fence, so he sat down and played one of Bates's dirges, very sad and rainy and appropriate. He didn't mind, if he could play what he liked, but even in this thing, which was supposed to be pleasure, it was nag, nag, nag all the way, and being told who he was supposed to like. For God's sake, how could they expect you to like their deadly stuff because they said it was good? You even had to take exams in it, this *pleasure*! What right had Dotty to say that this bluesy achy stuff was rubbish, when it was exactly how he felt, or that rave-ups were tripe? Who was *he* to say – God Almighty? Penn got more cheerful, playing for once without his mother yelling for deadliness instead of pop. He moved on to his mother's favourite loathes, and forgot about Arthur and the rain. It was as good as playing the harmonica in *Mathilda*, because he could do as he pleased. Cripes, all these years he had played, and always to order, for Dotty or his mother! I'm just a slave, he thought . . . do this, do that . . . what bliss if he could leave home . . . Arthur's wife was coming back on Thursday. She was deadliness again. Penn played a few bars of Chopin's funeral march.

'Why didn't you tell me you could play that thing?' Arthur said, padding out into the bar. 'We used to have music here – got the licence for it and all – till Joe packed it in. Saturday nights – it was great here. I could give you a job if you weren't under age. You're as good as Joe ever was.'

Penn scowled.

Arthur said, 'You don't look sixteen. If you hadn't told me, I'd have put you at eighteen.'

'Old West and Mitchell know how old I am.' Penn would have been quite prepared to turn himself into eighteen for Arthur's sake, if it hadn't been for the vigilance of the law. He would have fancied a job as a pub pianist, better than scrubbing.

'You come here when you're eighteen, and I'll take you on all right.'

'It's a dead easy way of earning money,' Penn said, wondering why he had never thought of it before. 'How much d'you get for playing for a night?'

'Oh, free drinks and a quid or two. Depends. Pity.' Arthur reflected a moment, and said, 'There's a crowd of weirdies used to come here for musical evenings. Folk-singing or something. They used the piano, but none of 'em played it as good as you. They had guitars as well, and a mouth-organ or two. There was a spot of trouble one night and they use the village hall now, Wednesday nights. They come round here first for a few crates of beer. You might get a job with them.'

Penn was interested.

Wednesday nights? Old Bates might like a spot of that, he thought. His dirges were mostly folk stuff. Penn had never found out yet where he got them from.

He asked him the next time he saw him.

'I get them out of the library. Books,' Bates explained. 'They're all in books.'

Penn had never heard of anyone using the library before. Not any of his friends.

'You want to try this old thing Arthur was talking about, then? Load of geezers singing? With beer,' he added, for incentive.

'I don't mind giving it a listen.'

They went, suspicious, sullen, and leaned against the door at the back of the hall. Penn was comforted by the length of hair. There was a man who sang who could scarcely see out. Penn couldn't see that there was anything in it for him, but he liked it. It had this thing that touched him when he played for Bates, that one played and sang to relieve something, to feel good, not for the sake of mastering a tortuous conglomeration of composer's fads for old Dotty's sake. For *pleasure*, for God's sake! Penn was jolted.

The audience was thin, but enthusiastic, joining in all the choruses. The long-haired man sang unaccompanied, but two others sang and played guitars, and another man played the harmonica. Penn found that a lot of the songs were Bates's; he could have joined in quite a lot of them if he had wanted. Not that he did want. He leaned against the doorpost in the dark outpost of the hall, superior, pulled against his will into the warmth, liking it, but resisting. His inside was going with it, but his face scowled. Bates was muttering under his breath, excited.

'This is my stuff,' he said.

'Yeah, well, they're public, aren't they?' Penn said witheringly. 'You said so. They're in the library.'

'I know, but—'

The long-haired man was introducing someone else, a girl. Penn's interest quickened. She was thin and frail-looking, with enormous sad eyes and long, straight, silver-blonde hair. Her voice was very clear, almost shrill, with a sadness that went with her looks.

'Ten thousand miles it is too far
To leave me here alone
Here I may lie, lament and cry . . .'

Penn stopped scowling, transfixed by the sword-edge of the girl's voice. He had never seen a bird as perfect as this one, so utterly desirable. She was like a piece of crystal, delicate, brittle, rare. He had never seen one like it. All the girls he knew were busty and thrusty and strong, all private giggles and shrieks, nudging and daring and passing notes. They had no reticence, brash and sniggering. But this little wispy thing, like a puff of breeze, her voice full of tears . . . Penn's eyes were wide open, hypnotized. When she was finished he could not say anything. Bates looked at him and he scowled.

He could not get her out of his head.

When they went home he said to Bates, very cautious, 'That bird wasn't bad.'

'What bird?' Bates said.

'Oh, cripes,' Penn said to himself. He felt spent and shattered and not all present. He did not know what to do.

Penn duly went back to school. Having been isolated in the Green Man all the holidays, Penn's natural gloom at returning to the deadly Beehive was lifted somewhat by the sight of Smeeton, and the thought of tangling with him once more.

'Haven't seen you down the river lately, Smeeton. You scared or something?'

'I've been working, thickhead. I'll be down the boat as soon as I fancy an evening's fishing, don't you worry.'

'I'll be there to help you aboard,' Penn said kindly. 'Just you tell me what night. I'll have everything ready for you.'

'I'll surprise you one of these days, Pennington,' Smeeton said.

'You surprise me all the time, Smeeton. That anyone

so disgusting can actually draw breath is a perpetual—'

'Soggy!'

They all scattered into their places. Soggy had the boys on one side of the classroom and the girls on the other, all the dullest, ugliest and spottiest specimens occupying the desks where the two sexes actually came together. The girl Penn had dated up to the end of last term, by name Rita Fairweather, occupied a desk next to the wall, and Penn had one against the window at the far side, which ranked them both, by Soggy's system, high in the sex-appeal stakes. Much Biro fluid had been expended by the girls in the Beehive on little notes and decorations declaring love for 'PP', but Penn, although he talked sex a lot like all the others, had privately – till now – thought girls pretty tedious. Not that he would have admitted this to anybody, except possibly to Bates. He had not given Rita a thought the whole holiday. In fact, the holiday had been a pleasant respite from the weekly date where Rita had spent most of his pocket-money for him on her never-ending passion for crisps and Coke and given nothing in return but a few salt'n'vinegar flavoured kisses on the back seat of the last bus. Penn, doing what he had thought were the right things, had been left unmoved. 'Give me a harmonica for company any day,' he said to Bates. And Bates, on his second can of Double Diamond, had sung:

'I wish I was a butterfly, I'd fly to my love's breast.
I wish I was a linnet, I would sing my love to rest.
I wish I was a nightingale, I'd sit and sing so clear,
I'd sing a song for you, false love, for once I loved
you dear.'

Penn didn't see it himself — then. But since the girl
with the voice he didn't know what he thought. Every
time he recalled her he felt weak in his stomach, as if
suffering from something physical. He could not tell
even Bates about this. Sometimes he thought the girl
was just a figment of his imagination, and that she had
never existed at all, but when, for a sort of try-out, he
said to Bates, 'That bird that sang, d'you reckon she was
any good?' Bates didn't say, 'What bird?' He said, 'Yeah.
She could sing all right. Not much to look at, though.'
And Penn felt stabbed again. Bates liked hunky big girls
when he thought about them at all. Penn, who had
never bothered about any of them, could not
understand why the little blonde kept fluttering in his
inside.

'Coming events,' Soggy intoned. 'Dates to fix in your
thick heads for the summer term . . . don't bring me any
excuses later, saying I didn't warn you. I'm warning you
now. First and most important, upper school social event
for pupils and parents Saturday, May the tenth, in aid of

the Common Room extension fund. Compulsory for you lot. Parents to be dragged along if possible. Mr Robert Tate is coming to sing for us.'

Everyone groaned, as a matter of form.

'What group's he with, sir?' someone asked.

'He sings,' Soggy explained, 'properly.'

Everyone groaned again.

'I repeat, compulsory attendance,' Soggy said. 'May the tenth, five pm. Everyone got it?'

Penn's faint flicker of goodwill drooped and died. His last term, true to form, stretched like grey, spent chewing-gum, tasteless, useless and tedious, into the hazy horizons of his seventeenth summer. He looked out of the window and saw the glazed walls of the new buildings shining in the sunshine, the hotchpotch of roofs beyond and, through the gap between Langford's chimney and the slate roof of the Methodist church, a shimmer of soft blue that was the sea. The tiny gap of shimmer made him feel physically ill for a moment. To get out, to get shot of the lot of them . . . To what? To where? How? The dirty—

'Pennington!'

He refocused. 'Sir?'

'I'll give you two days to get your hair cut.'

Penn felt the waters rising.

★   ★   ★

In the lunch-hour, closeted with Mr Crocker in the music room, Penn revealed – not by saying anything, but merely through the way he played – that he had done no practising since leaving school at the end of last term. Little Mr Crocker danced with rage. Penn felt sorry for him.

'What can I do with you? What use are you to me? To anyone? To yourself? Why do I trouble? I ask myself over and over, why do I trouble?'

Penn felt, very faintly, guilty. Mr Crocker did trouble. He was the only one. He shifted on the stool and stared morosely at the music. Mr Crocker slipped another sheet down over the one he was looking at, an ominous affair headed 'Andante and Rondo Capriccioso' by Felix Mendelssohn.

'Look at that.'

Penn looked at Dotty suspiciously.

'You have one more term with me, Pennington. Why should we waste it? I understand from the rest of the staff that you waste a good deal of your time here. Well, I thought, not with me he won't. I am ambitious for you, you see, Pennington.'

'But, sir—'

'There's to be a music festival here in Northend towards the end of June. I've entered you for the Open

Solo Pianoforte. The Andante and Rondo Capriccioso is the set piece.'

Penn stared at Dotty, aghast. 'The *Open*?'

'You are perfectly capable of playing this piece. So why not? We will work very hard this term, you and I.'

'But I don't want—'

'I'm sorry,' Dotty said. 'But to borrow a favourite word from Mr Marsh, it's compulsory.'

He leaned on the piano. 'It was discussed at a staff meeting. Everyone agreed that it would be a very good thing, both for yourself and for the school, if you could do well in this competition. It was also agreed that you waste a good deal of time while you are in school. So, with a little cooperation from all concerned, we drew up a timetable for you, Pennington, to make sure that you get all the practice in that you need. It's arranged so that you get at least three hours in every day. An hour at lunch-time, an hour after school, when I shall work with you, and various other periods during each day – for example, Miss Harrington is generously prepared to forgo the pleasure of your company in her Religious Education lessons on Tuesday and Thursday; Mr Peach tells me you're banned from the metalwork shop, which gives you an hour and forty minutes on Wednesday afternoon, and Mr Marsh seems to think Current Events could get along without you very well – that's

Tuesday again. A splendid day, Tuesday – you will get over three and a half hours.'

He expounded, at great length, every minute of this formidable timetable, while Penn sat looking at the music, resistance setting in like arthritis, stiffening his whole body. There was no escape. It was a gigantic revenge, plotted by the gleeful, scheming staff to sabotage his indolent summer.

'All this time wasted during the winter on soccer,' Crocker went on scornfully. 'Hours tossed away! Every time I tried to get a lunch-hour Matthews had got you out on the field. And then that broken arm – six weeks gone! Well, now, you can make up for it this term. Sit up! *Sit up!* Let's get the cramp out of those fingers. Twenty minutes of this, please.' Another sheet of deadliness, close and black, slipped down before his eyes. 'With the metronome at . . .' Penn groaned out loud. Crocker brought a ruler down with a crack across his knuckles and Penn jumped. He started to play. He had a feeling that he was sliding under again, the rapid clock of the metronome counting his pulse as he drowned in a sea of deadliness.

'This crummy concert, with Mr Robert Tate. We've decided to do something about it.'

They were packing up after afternoon school, and

Maxwell, a prefect from 5A, banged for attention on the desk.

'We reckon we can string together an evening's entertainment that'll put old Tate in the shade. After all, we want this blooming Common Room extension and nobody's going to come and listen to old septuagenarian Tate bleating his hey nonny, are they? Even the parents aren't that far past it.'

Penn, seeing more work in the offing, attempted to slip nonchalantly out of the door, but Maxwell caught him by the arm.

'It's you I want, oaf.'

'I'm strictly the old Beethoven, Bach and blooming Brahms,' Penn said. 'You ask Dotty. Even farther back than Tate.'

'Look here,' Maxwell said. 'We aren't interested in that lot any more than you are. It's Bates I want to know about.'

'Bates!'

'Rumour has it he's got a repertoire of soul—'

'Why don't you ask him?' Penn was grinning.

'He'll shut up like a clam, you know that. You've got to work on him for us.'

'It's the old beer he sings for, not me.'

'How do you mean?'

'He has to get loosened up. And he won't do it in

public. To make him do it in public you'll have to get him really oiled.'

Maxwell looked a little dubious. A bright boy, right-half to Penn's centre, he was a friend of Penn's. 'We can't have him drunk, you fool. There must be a happy medium in this. He just wants a little something to loosen the inhibitions?'

'That's it.'

'Well, I don't see why that shouldn't be arranged. You'd play the old harmonica for him? He wouldn't be alone, after all. Could you talk him into it, do you think?'

'I can try.'

'He's good? Worth the trouble?'

'He is a darned sight better than old Tate.'

'We'll have an audition after school next week. I'll lay the beer on. It could be all right, this affair. We don't want the parents to think we're so pathetic that we can't give Tate any competition. 5B's got a group that's not bad, and there's Finnigan's trumpet, and Midwinter's monologue, cleaned up a bit, and you on the old joanna, if it's the stuff you do in the Common Room, not Dotty's murk. I can leave Bates to you, can I? Talk him into it . . .'

Bates looked gloomy as soon as the subject was introduced. 'What, me stand up there? I can't sing, anyway.'

'Well, I'm your manager now, and you'll do what I say. I've signed you on.'

'What'll I sing, for heaven's sake?'

'What's wrong with "The Butcher Boy"? Good meaty stuff.'

Bates went crimson. 'It's a girl's song. They'd roll up, me standing up there . . . "I wish I was a maid again" . . .'

Penn considered. It had never made him want to roll up, Bates's tale of the wronged girl. But, spotty old Bates . . . He looked at him thoughtfully. Of course, it was a bit daft, when you came to think of it, spotty old Bates singing:

'I wish my baby it was born
And smiling on its daddy's knee
And me, poor girl, to be dead and gone
With the long green grass growing over me.'

But he had never laughed. Penn could not understand why.

He said raspingly, 'Who wanted to sing on the telly the other night, then? Who wanted to sing for his living? Where's the old ambition? If you can't stand up and sing for a few dozy old parents you jolly well *ought* to be a crummy girl.'

Penn had already decided that he wasn't going to

play the piano, not for anybody's sake, but Bates was ruddy well going to sing. Bates, who never did anything at school but sit in the corner staring out of the window all day, was going to get up on the platform and sing. He, Patrick Pennington, had made up his mind.

If it had been a concert forced on them by the staff he would have been as uncooperative as possible, but as it was one organized by Maxwell to do down Hey Nonny Tate, he was prepared to show willing.

Bates, who was sitting on *Mathilda*'s bunk when this conversation took place, opened his mouth to voice another protest, but stopped in mid-word, staring at the suddenly darkened hatch.

Penn turned round just as Smeeton jumped. Smeeton, in his enthusiasm, had not stopped to balance himself and fell upon Penn in a sprawl of arms and legs, from which Penn detached himself more quickly than his attacker. But already the hatch had darkened again, and first Fletcher then Gary and Gerry Green dropped through, like parachutists, Bates thought. Bates pulled his legs up on to the bunk and sat in the corner, cradling his knees in his arms, watching the rapid transformation of the small cuddy take place before his unsurprised eyes, utter chaos shattering the domestic peace like fireworks through a letter-box. Penn did most of the damage, flailing like a harpooned whale under the mass attack, so that table, beer, and paraffin lamp all went flying, wood splintering and glass shattering. Grunts, cries, and breathless invective punctuated the graver noises of destruction. Bates sighed, and felt the old smack rock as if a squall had hit her. The teacups chinked on their hooks, and the tins in the lockers rattled faintly; the rusty gimbals swung at the impact of a boot, the empty kettle clattered round its compound. Bates heard Penn's voice from below, muffled and *in extremis*, and gradually the heaving of limbs slackened off and Smeeton's voice could be heard, triumphant, from beneath Fletcher's posterior: 'Let me get up, Fletcher, you louse. We've done for him.' Bates peered down. He saw Penn's eyes glittering. Bates grinned. Penn started to move again, but Smeeton, quick as a stoat, picked up the lamp-glass, which was broken across the middle, and brought the jagged edges sharply up to Penn's face. Penn, already moving forward, tasted the blood on his lip.

'You scurvy—' Penn was almost weeping at his defeat, the words brimming on his tongue. The glass had stopped him. Smeeton, half alarmed by the blood, half exhilarated, sat back, nervously passing the glass from hand to hand. Penn raised himself on his elbows, feeling very ill from his treatment.

'We thought we'd go fishing,' Smeeton said, slightly

uncertain. 'Didn't we?' He appealed to his henchmen, who were sitting on the bunks. 'We thought we'd go out for the evening.'

'Yeah,' they all said.

There was a pause, which seemed to emphasize Smeeton's unfamiliarity with victory, and Fletcher said, indicating Penn, 'What'll we do with him, then?'

'He won't make any more trouble, not from the look of him. You don't want any more, Pennington, do you? You've only to say.'

Penn said nothing, groping for a handkerchief.

'Come on, get the engine started, then,' Smeeton said to Fletcher. 'Get the gear on board. You two stay down here or you'll get pasted again,' he added to Penn and Bates.

The invading party departed up the hatchway, and could be heard thumping around on deck, unloading gear out of the dinghy. Penn went on lying on the floor. Bates unwound himself and sat up, looking dubiously at Penn.

'You want a beer or something?'

Penn told him, curtly, that he didn't.

Bates shrugged. 'Fag?' Penn shook his head. In the hold the engine started up with a series of backfires, and the fumes filtered through, blue and filmy. The smack vibrated, and all the crockery started to shiver again, and the beer cans trembled in their case. Bates started to tidy up, gathering up the bits of lamp, stepping over Penn. He heard the mooring go with a splash, and the old smack made a juddering circle and set off down the river. The engine was at full throttle, rough and strangled, coughing unhappily at frequent intervals, and the cuddy was filled with the clatter and banging of loose gear on deck, of halyards swinging on the mast and blocks tapping. Smeeton was singing. Bates looked up and saw the summer evening sky, clear and inviting, sliding past. The boat seemed to be moving very fast. He looked at Penn, whose handkerchief now looked very bloody, and said, 'Are you OK?'

'Oh, get stuffed,' Penn said.

Bates went and stood in the hatchway, leaning his elbows on the deck, watching the quays of Moorham slipping into sight, and the jetty where the battle was first joined. The houses on the quay, facing south, were bathed in a golden light, the long shadows flung behind them. Bates could smell summer, and felt perfectly content. He started to sing under the racket of the engine, watching the boat's shadow moving down the river. The tide hurried *Mathilda* seaward. The sea-walls moved back, fading against the fading sky, and the sea spread out, gold and smooth and glittering. The ease of *Mathilda*'s passage – in spite of the din – enchanted Bates . . .

'The salt seaweed was in her hair
Lowlands, lowlands away . . .
And then I knew my love was dead . . .'

Two beer cans, tossed away by the company at the helm, bobbed away, shooting metallic stars. Smeeton was laughing. The boat was going too fast for the fishing, but nobody cared, least of all Bates.

'When he was dead and laid in grave
Her heart was struck with sorrow.
Oh mother, mother, make my bed,
For I shall die tomorrow.'

The engine, throwing out clouds of thick blue smoke, made a curious choking noise and stopped. In the startling silence Bates heard his own voice, and stopped as abruptly.

'Go and kick it, Fletcher,' Smeeton ordered.

'Give it some beer,' Gerry suggested.

'Go and get Penn,' Smeeton said. 'He can ruddy well work his passage. He always thinks he knows all about it.'

They came aft. Bates retreated and said to Penn, 'They want you to fix the engine.'

Penn said, 'They can——'

'Pennington, you louse, get up here,' Fletcher said, bending down to peer through the hatch. 'Get this engine going again. We don't want to get our hands dirty.'

Penn went, hunched and muttering, blinking at the sunset, swallowing blood. Bates saw them go down the aft hatch, and presently heard the familiar noises of the flywheel being turned over, and Penn arguing with Fletcher as to the reason for the failure. Bates did not care. He stood in the hatch again, squinting at the strange gold gloss that was the sea, the smack's shadow drawn long and dark across the water. She was drifting, slowly turning her bows to the outgoing tide, rolling as she came across the swell. There was no land in sight, the low sea-walls lost in the encroaching haze. The sun lay on the horizon like a huge red buoy. Bates was touched by the austere beauty, never having known such loveliness before.

'The fuel's not coming through——'

'Clean the carburettor, then.'

'. . . can't see a thing down here and you've broken the lamp.'

Fragments of altercation, muffled, did not disturb

Bates's reverie. He was looking down the bleached sweep of *Mathilda*'s decks and out to sea, where dusk was rapidly tarnishing the impossible gold. The smack had settled herself, bows into the tide, and was going away from the shore stern first. The shadow of her mast was ten miles long, to the horizon. A violet haze ate up the sun, the shadow vanished, and the sea was cold, grey and unkind, the change taking place in a matter of seconds. Bates was amazed, hurt. He went below again and lay on the bunk, 'Poor old Penn,' he thought. He started to sing.

Smeeton came down, looking annoyed, and said, 'Any candles on this old heap? Penn said there were some in a locker.'

Bates groped for them and handed them over. Smeeton retired. Flickers of light came and went, and hammering, and the hopeless noises of a goaded engine trying and failing, to an accompaniment of swearing. Half an hour later the smack hit something with a crack that sent all the gathered crockery shooting back on to the floor again. She lifted and came down with a jar that Bates felt come out of the top of his head. He went up on deck.

'We're aground,' Penn was saying. 'Ruddy fine skipper you are, Smeeton.'

'What do you mean, aground?' Smeeton said, staring

over the side. Sea surrounded them to infinity on all sides, gleaming now in the first light of a half-moon.

'On the bottom, pinhead. On the sand. What are you going to do about it?'

Penn, holding on to the shrouds, was ready when the swell dropped the smack again, but the shock sent Smeeton sprawling. Penn laughed. Bates looked at him cautiously. He knew that to go aground in a smack as frail as *Mathilda*, even in a calm sea, was no joke, but Penn was laughing.

'What are you going to do?' Penn asked Smeeton again.

'Oh, I don't know,' Smeeton said crossly. The failure of the engine had destroyed his confidence.

'Anchor,' Penn said. He sat on the coaming of the hold, his elbows on his knees, and looked out over the shoal, fingering the congealing blood on his lip. The shoal was marked by a large area of breaking water in an otherwise calm sea. 'You've put this old boat in a nasty situation, Smeeton,' he said conversationally. 'You ought to do something about it.'

Smeeton looked at Penn and saw by the set of his shoulders that Penn was no longer to be ordered about. He said to Fletcher, 'Go and put the anchor out.' He paused until Fletcher and the Green brothers had tramped away to sort out the anchor, and said, 'What do we do, then?'

Penn said, 'I don't know about you, but I'm turning in.' And he went below and installed himself in the lee bunk, the only one that was comfortable when the old smack, drying out on the sand, lay down on her side.

Chapter Four

BATES, ALTHOUGH HE knew all about the shoals out at sea, had never met one in the flesh before. While the rest of them slept, Penn soundly and Smeeton and Co. very uncomfortably on the floor and deck, Bates went for a walk. He walked on a hard ridge of unmarked sand, virgin as arctic snow, shining like slate under the hard moonlight, with the sea all round him and waders twittering eerily on the fringes of the water. It was so strange that he could hardly believe it, although he told himself that it happened every night, and was only a few miles from home. The night was sharp, with a rising wind. Clouds started to drift over the moon and, standing beside the stranded smack, Bates could hear the noise of the wind whining in the shrouds. The loose halyards swung out in restive arcs, slapping the deck. When the water started to come back it was no longer smooth; it broke on the sand with considerable force, and Bates could see the white crests spitting in the darkness, even where the water was deep.

When the tide was nearly back to the smack, he climbed on board and went below to Penn. Smeeton and Fletcher, propped uncomfortably on the tilting floor, were only dozing, and mumbled at him, but Penn was deeply asleep, sprawled out on his back.

Bates shook him. He had no faith in Smeeton.

'The water's nearly back. What are we going to do? The wind's come up as well.'

Penn grumbled into consciousness, and lay listening to the restless noises all about him. 'Ask Smeeton,' he said to Bates. 'It's his trip.'

'You're always making out you're an engineer,' Smeeton said. 'If you can't make the engine go, what can I do about it?'

'The engine won't go – you needn't worry about that any longer,' Penn said. 'She'll have to sail out, if she's going at all.'

'Sail!'

Penn shut his eyes again. 'There's sails in the forepeak.'

There was a long silence. Bates sat down on the bunk by Penn's knees, anxious. 'Penn,' he said, 'Smeeton can't sail.'

'He should have thought of that before he got us into this mess.'

'What are you going to do, Penn?' Bates insisted.

'I'm just keeping a stiff upper lip,' Penn said.

'It's no joke!'

'No, it isn't. It's true.'

'Oh, stow it, Penn. It's bad. You know it is.'

Penn did know, although he shut his eyes again and did not move. He could hear the wind through the rotted rigging, and the slap of the water on the hull, and knew that the old boat was going to take a pounding that might well open her up before she floated. They had no dinghy with them, nor flares, no life-saving equipment of any kind. He judged that they were about five miles off shore. He thought, with luck and an ingoing tide, he might swim that, but he knew none of the others could. He was sorry for Bates.

Smeeton got up without saying anything and went up on deck, where he could be heard muttering to the others and thumping about. They opened the forehatch and Penn could hear them looking for the sails, stumbling about in the dark. The smack was beginning to shudder as the force of the deepening water got under her, buffeting and shouldering the rotten timbers. Yes, thought Penn, it was bad. But he felt exhilarated more than frightened. Bates shook him again.

'Penn, you aren't going to leave it to Smeeton, are you?'

Penn was touched. 'No. I don't want to drown. But let him sweat! He deserves to.'

'It'll be all right?'

'Yes, of course, you fool.'

Penn did not move until he felt the crack as the smack's keel left the bottom and dropped for the first time. It was ominous. He rolled his feet off on to the floor and sat combing his hair. The smack was wallowing horribly from side to side, like a cow struggling in a bog. Every few seconds she bumped, and every minute or so a larger wave would lift and drop her with a sickening crack. He went up on deck, Bates following anxiously at his heels.

Gary and Gerry, who knew more about boats than Smeeton, had got the headsails on, but were now being sick over the side, while the unleashed canvas flogged and cracked dangerously across the foredeck. Smeeton and Fletcher, standing over the anchor chain, were in danger of being flailed overboard. Penn went to the mast and dropped the sails.

'Have you pulled up on that anchor?' he asked.

'Can't move it,' Smeeton muttered. In the darkness his face was a white, petrified blur. The water was slopping up over the foredeck, moving apparently in all directions with a malicious strength. The sand was marked by a white, blowing spray. Penn looked at it, and was frightened. They were alone with their crank boat and there was no one to help them. He was the only one who knew anything about it – and he didn't know much. It was cold, and he was soaked already by the spray.

He said to Fletcher, 'Go and see if you can find some sheets for those sails. They're useless without. Rope, I mean. Bring up anything you can find.' He elbowed Smeeton out of his way, and grasped the anchor chain where it came over the fairlead.

'Get behind me and pull when I pull. When she comes up, heave.' Smeeton was just a weed. Penn got his hands round the chain, bracing one leg against the bulwarks. The smack rolled and the stem lifted. 'Now!' Penn flung himself on the chain and pulled in about a fathom before it stopped him. Smeeton had the sense to get the slack round the samson-post. The smack snubbed up with a snatching, chafing motion, slewing round on her shuddering stern. The water came over with sharp thuds, the smack dropping on the hard sand, sawing at her anchor. The shocks of her pounding went up Penn's spine like explosions. He had never guessed it would be as bad as this, in spite of what he had said. Bates was crying.

'Again!' he said to Smeeton, getting hold of the anchor chain.

It came in in snatches, a foot at a time. Penn got as much as he could, until exhaustion stopped him, and Smeeton feverishly made it fast as it came, sliding the slack back down the hause-hole. Dragged forcibly towards the deep water, *Mathilda* began to ride, dropping with less force, gradually freeing her stern. Penn went below to see how much water she was making, but there was none over the floorboards, which cheered him considerably, although he could hear it swilling in the bilges. He knew her pump was useless. He rested for a moment in the hatchway, biting the side of his thumb, looking out into the darkness. All he could see was breaking crests, the south-westerly wind kicking into the tide, knocking the tops off the making waves, driving the smack, if it could, farther out to sea. To sail back would mean beating into it. The mouth of the river was unlit, and full of shoals, but they could not wait for daylight, because by then the tide would have turned again, and an old smack like *Mathilda* would not make it against both wind and tide together, however skilfully she was sailed. They had to go now, whether they liked it or not. Penn stood a little longer, licking the blood out of his lip, which was bleeding again and stinging with the salt. So much for Smeeton's evening fishing-party, he thought. He reckoned that by the time they made base, if they ever did, he'd have Smeeton crying for mercy.

The mainsail was lashed on the boom, and Penn got Gerry and Gary to shake it out and start tying down the reefs.

'It's probably full of holes. Any of you used it lately?'

They shook their heads. 'We always go on the engine,' Gerry said. They were prepared to do anything Penn said. Gerry had reeved on some makeshift sheets to the headsails. Penn changed the knots from grannies to bowlines, and took the ends back aft and gave them to Bates.

'She's got to pay off the right way when the anchor comes out, or we'll just go back on the sand again. When I shout at you, cleat this down here, tight as you can and put the tiller over this way. Point her like this.' He pointed. He had to shout at Bates, both crouching on the deck, hunched against the spray. 'I'll come back as soon as the anchor is out. It might take some time.' He knew the theory, but not much else. 'We could do with Jim here right now,' he said to Bates.

He got Gerry and Gary to stand by the mainsail, ready to haul, and Fletcher on the staysail. 'Smeeton, you can help me with the anchor.' They were all falling over each other, flung about by the violent motion of the smack. The water kept coming over in dollops. There was no point any more in ducking to miss it; they were soaked through. Penn went to the anchor and picked up the chain again. 'Ready?' he asked Smeeton.

It took twenty minutes to get the anchor. Penn swore at Smeeton with what snatches of breath he could spare, and swore at the grating fairlead when the chain inched back, and at the water swilling through the bulwarks. Everyone but Penn was sick. When Smeeton retched up all over the sliding, clanking chain he was trying to make fast, Penn laughed.

When the anchor came out at last, and Gerry and Gary sweated up the sails, the old smack lay down and ran, more under the water than over it. The loose chain ran with a crash into the bulwarks, Smeeton frantically chasing it. Fletcher and Gary dangled on the ends of the halyards, groping for their cleats; Fletcher had lost his balance and hit the corner of the hatch with such force that he was doubled up and useless. Penn stumbled over him, shouting at Bates, 'Free off! Free off!'

'Which way?' Bates sobbed.

'For cripes' sake!' Penn clawed his way along the lee deck, knee-deep in water. It was pandemonium, the loose jib flogging with guts enough to pull the forestay out. Penn got the tiller off Bates and eased it, freeing off so that the wind was more on the beam. The smack got up, and the water poured out along her scuppers.

'Get that sheet! Pull it in! Here, let me have it!' With his thigh to the tiller, Penn hauled in the flogging jib, brute strength capturing it. Bates wound the sheet frantically round the cleat.

'Go and find a compass, for God's sake! Tell Smeeton to look out for shoal water, or buoys or something. If we go aground again——!' It would be curtains, at the rate *Mathilda* was travelling, but he didn't say so to Bates. He was shivering, although the sweat was running off him after getting the anchor. He thought he was as scared as Smeeton looked, but hadn't as much time to think about it. Thank God, Gerry and Gary had made the halyards fast. How long they would hold was another matter. Any of the gear was likely to give up at any moment, mast and hull included. Most of the crew had given up already, retching up what was left in their stomachs. Penn, tonguing his lip, was fiercely satisfied. They had hurt him last night. He wasn't used to being beaten.

The way into the river was up into the wind. The compass did not help much, without a chart, and there was no chart on board. The sea was very rough, but Penn knew that the shoals would be marked by even rougher water. They all stared for it, blinking through the spray, aware that it mattered more than anyone was prepared to admit in words. *Mathilda* shouldered through the waves, plunging into troughs with shuddering cracks that set all her seams weeping. The floorboards below were awash. Fletcher, almost out for the count, went and lay down, groaning, and the water broke over his dangling hands, swilling a sour stench of old paraffin, fish and beer through the black cuddy. Smeeton went to look for a leadline, and was sick again. He hadn't the strength to climb back out of the cuddy, and sat on the bottom step of the companion-way, moaning softly to himself. Bates went to have a look, and the sight cheered him immensely.

'It's like one of those old emigrant ships,' he said to Penn, 'that engraving for "Botany Bay".' 'Botany Bay' was one of his songs.

'Yes, pity it's only three miles, and not ten thousand. Go and ask Smeeton why he's not fishing.'

Bates did so. Smeeton didn't reply. Bates came back and said, 'There's enough water down there. He doesn't even have to move.'

Penn hoped privately that it wouldn't increase. A faint light behind them suggested that dawn might come in time to show them the mouth of the river. Having come so far, Penn was feeling more confident, amazed that the old ruin had held together in such conditions.

'You know,' he said to Bates, 'we ought to have tried sailing her more often. Not in this sort of weather – I mean on nice days. Just a bit of wind. I never thought she'd do this.' He wiped his hair out of his eyes, squinting ahead. 'We'd better go about. I think that's shallow ahead.'

He put the tiller over. *Mathilda* was an old cow to tack, unbalanced with her reefed mainsail. He made a hash of it and had to sail again, the line of white foam unpleasantly close. The second time she hung in stays for what seemed a century, but at last, when he was beginning to feel the panic getting hold, she paid off and went away on the skirts of the white foam, heading for deep water. Penn wiped his face, shaking. He had never been scared like this before, he realized, not for anything so important – only for people sometimes, his father and Soggy and the magistrate, which was different. He was pleased that he had kept his head. It made him feel strange, that he could enjoy what was happening at the same time as feeling scared to death. Not like Smeeton, giving in, like a jelly. They'd be lucky if they made it, with *Mathilda* rotten as a wormy apple, but now he thought they would.

'What about it, Bates?' he said. 'She's not so past it, is she?'

Bates gave a green smile.

'We'll sail her again. I didn't know she would.'

If there was a nice day, he thought, they could lay off school and have a trip out.

When it got light they were off the mouth of the river, where the water was always worse than anywhere else, even in good weather. *Mathilda* rattled about, groaning and straining, long splits opening out in her staysail. She was full of water. Penn gave the tiller to Bates and went forward. Gerry and Gary were sitting on the forehatch.

'Enjoy yourselves?' Penn asked.

He put his head in the hatch and shouted down the cuddy, 'Smeeton, come up here! And Fletcher.'

'Lay off!' Smeeton muttered.

'Why should I? I'm going to court-martial you. You can get ashore up on the mud here. Bates and I are sick of your stench.'

Smeeton didn't move, until Penn started to come down the companion-way, then he got up and crawled up into the air. His face was grey.

'Best cure for seasickness in the world,' Penn said, pointing to a hard mud spit that came out from the sea-wall ahead of them. 'Land. It'll do you good, Smeeton, believe me – I'm doing you a favour. We can't go too close in, mind you – just close enough for you to jump.'

If there had been any fight in them at all they could just have easily turned on him and shoved him out on the mud. But Penn's confidence smothered them, and they were sick enough to want to go. They jumped when Penn said jump, and landed in four feet of dark, cold water. Penn stood at the tiller and watched them flounder up the spit. He felt marvellous. He laughed, loud enough for them to hear, and Bates sat smiling and saying, 'That was terrific, Penn. You do have good ideas.'

Penn didn't feel so marvellous when he got home.

'Oh, so you've condescended to drop in for some breakfast?' his mother said. 'It's nice to see you when you're just passing by. Do sit down and make yourself at home.'

'I'll get washed.'

'We've hot and cold in every room in this hotel.' She flounced round from the cooker, her lips tight. Penn waited for the onslaught, weary and hating her. He took his hand away from his face and she saw his lip and her expression changed.

'How d'you get that? Fighting?'

'Smeeton had a lump of glass.'

'God in heaven, what a mess! Go and run it under the cold tap. It's just like your father had that time outside the Plough and Sail when young Billy knocked his beer over and they all went berserk. He's still got the mark now. And I reckon you'll have, too, unless you get it stitched. You'd better go down to the surgery.'

'Oh, Ma, it'll wait till tonight.'

'You'll do what I say for a change! You've missed the school bus as it is. Get a move on now! You choose to do these things, don't you? You choose to stay out all night and get slashed up fighting with that load of layabouts, then you take the consequences, my lad. Fat lot of good your education has done you so far. All what I fought for to get for you, and you're still as big a yob as the rest of them—'

Penn shoved his way past and out of the kitchen, slamming the door. He went upstairs, almost in tears, all his pleasant feelings of triumph over both Smeeton and the sea – especially the sea – shattered and scattered and obliterated. He locked himself in the bathroom and contemplated his lip, scowling, in the mirror. It looked awful. He cleaned himself up very slowly and got a clean white shirt out of the airing cupboard and fetched his tie. He hated his mother bitterly. When he got downstairs again he ate his breakfast with difficulty and his mother railed at him without stopping, on and on, so that he got the sour impression that the house was wired up for canned invective, like a restaurant for canned music, and if his mother had gone out it would still have gone on and on. Only he had no way of switching it off. He could only depart.

'To the doctor's,' his mother shouted after him. 'Else I'll get your father on to you.'

★ ★ ★

The surgery was full of smelly, yelling babies and stupid women, and nothing to read but *Woman's Own* and *Country Life*. He read all the problems at the back of the women's papers, until the doctor buzzed for him.

'What did you do to get this?' the doctor asked, prodding ominously.

'I met a piece of glass coming the other way.'

'Young louts, wasting our time. You deserve all you get . . .' He treated Penn with marked lack of tenderness, so that Penn squirmed and swore. Halfway through, old Miss Marble, the district nurse, came in and said, 'If you're going to school after, Patrick, I can give you a lift as far as Parkfield. I've got a confinement there.'

Penn had already decided that such treatment as he was getting warranted a day off, but the doctor said, with a sadistic smile, 'It's your day, Pat, obviously.' Penn guessed that he was referring to Miss Marble's notorious driving: many people decided that they were going in the opposite direction when Miss Marble offered them a lift. 'You're perfectly fit to go to school,' he added, reading Penn's intentions. 'I'm sorry. Don't smile, that's all.' He grinned. Penn had no intention of smiling.

He went outside and got into Miss Marble's Mini, fastening the safety belt carefully.

'What have you been doing? Fighting?' Miss Marble asked brightly. He scowled.

'If you didn't frown all the time, Patrick, you'd be quite good-looking. How's the piano playing going? I hear you're very good.'

Penn grunted, wishing he'd hitchhiked.

'Miss Sparrow was wanting someone to play for her on Saturday mornings, for her dancing classes in the village hall. She asked me if I knew anyone. Would you fancy that? She'd pay you ten bob, I expect.'

'No,' said Penn. If the girls had been sixteen or so, he'd have said yes, but they weren't.

'I thought you'd say that. What a shame! You have so much to give, dear, with a talent like that. Really, Patrick, you ought to pull yourself together and start using your time more responsibly . . .'

The old bag, because she'd delivered them all, thought she could do the God Almighty, just like Soggy and Stacker . . . He pulled off the safety belt.

'If you put me down at the next crossing, I can get the bus,' he said.

'But I can take you on to Parkfield, dear. It will be quicker for you.' She went straight on past the turning, and overtook a lorry on a blind bend. Penn fastened the safety belt again quickly. 'I'm surprised they let you grow your hair so long at the Beehive, Patrick. I would have thought they had rules about that sort of thing . . .'

Penn shut his eyes and felt himself shrink. His outside felt hard, like shell, and his inside all churning, like the slosh through the window of a washing-machine. He remembered the sea, and the salt crusty to the tongue, the feeling of exhilaration, old *Mathilda* beating and flogging into the wind. Then he remembered the school smell of sweat and ink and dust, and the yellow keyboard of the Bechstein, all his for three and a half hours, and Soggy's eyes, cold and sarcastic.

Soggy gave him a detention for being late without a good excuse. He could see with his own eyes that Penn's explanation about going to the doctor's was true, but he chose not to accept it.

'I'm working to rule,' Soggy said. Penn knew that it was because of his hair. 'I'll give you till next Monday, Pennington,' he said. And Penn thought, With any luck, next Monday I'll get the sack.

Next Monday a staff meeting was held, with Pennington's hair on the agenda. Mr Peach, an irredeemable gambler, had run a book in the staff room on the effect of Soggy's ultimatum to Pennington, and had made a profit of thirty bob. The sight of Pennington's hair in assembly, falling thick and shining to his shoulders as he played a Bach prelude to fill in a technical hitch (Stacker having lost his glasses), had made Mr Peach's day. Mr Matthews, the games master, was the only one to be equally satisfied by the result. He had won a pound off Mr Peach. He had not considered that his money had been in any danger at all. 'If they think Pennington's going to step down now,' he said to Peach on Friday, 'after the whole thing has been made into an issue, they don't know Pennington. He's as pig-headed as they come. Fighting spirit and all that – why else is he so good at soccer? Because he's aggressive and dirty. He wants to blast the opposition off the field. And what do they do in this cock-eyed school? Sit him at a piano all day! Marsh has no more idea of how to handle a character like Pennington than fly in the air.'

'Well, let's face it, the piano is the only thing he's any good at, games apart.'

'Unfortunately for Pennington, yes.'

The whole school was now familiar with the strains of Mendelssohn's Rondo Capriccioso, or the old Capritch, as Penn's friends referred to it. Penn, unsupervised in a small practice-room for a good deal of his generous playing time, could not be trusted to keep on working – Crocker, calling in on him unexpectedly, had found him reading a paperback entitled *Sexual Permissiveness in the American Campus*, and had therefore insisted that Penn do his practice on the grand piano in the hall, where, if he stopped, he would be reported immediately by any one of several masters who would be teaching within earshot. This ruse was not popular with those forced to listen, many of whom found a solid hour of double octave scales a tedious background to their own voices, but it had the desired effect. Even now, the staff meeting was being conducted to the distant echoes of a Beethoven Sonata. To those members of the staff not particularly interested in Pennington's hair, the music was having a distinctly soporific effect.

'We can't go on ignoring this,' Mr Stack said. 'Others are following suit, and there's a limit to what's acceptable. Pennington reached that some weeks ago.'

'Pennington's been the limit ever since he first came here,' someone remarked.

'Yes, but we have only another two months of Pennington,' Mr Stack pointed out, to the accompaniment of several interjections of relief. 'We can surely handle this without actually making an issue of it?'

'An issue has been made of it already, by Mr Marsh,' Said Matthews.

'Am I supposed to accept Pennington's hair without comment, then?' Soggy asked acidly. 'If I had my way, I'd cane the living daylights out of him, but as our governors – God help us – consider this unenlightened,

95

I would be grateful for any alternative constructive suggestions anyone can make – including you, Matthews.'

'I'm not concerned,' Matthews said. 'I only know that Pennington will get sacked before he'll get his hair cut, the way he feels at present.'

'And much as we'd all quite like to see the back of him, I'm not sacking him at this stage,' said Mr Stack. 'With parents like his it's just not worth it. They'll have it in the newspapers immediately and the school will just be a laughing-stock – quite the last thing we want. But I agree with Mr Marsh, we can't ignore the whole business, much as we'd like to. Loss of privileges, possibly? Extra work—'

'He's already lost all his dinner-hours and an hour after school every day,' Matthews said, beginning to feel like fighting for Penn.

'But not his games,' Mr Marsh said, his eyes gleaming. 'Not his swimming and his athletics and his PE – which I understand he actually enjoys. The only subject, Mr Matthews – if you can call it a subject – which he would be unhappy to miss. I suggest, Mr Stack, that Pennington is stopped from games until he gets his hair cut.'

Mr Stack looked at Matthews, and dropped his eyes doubtfully. 'Well—'

'That's extremely unfair to me!' Matthews said hotly. 'And to the school, too! We've got a whole list of fixtures for the term, and he's in just about every one of them! And there's the swimming gala next month – we're all set for the cup if—'

'Well, if it's that important, it's up to you to see that he gets his hair cut,' Soggy said.

'Up to me! But *I* haven't made an issue of it, have I? I don't care if his hair is down to his backside if he wins.'

'It's a matter of principle, Matthews,' Stack said wearily.

'Sir, you know Pennington as well as I do! He won't get it cut now that it's been blown up into something on the agenda of a staff meeting, not even if you take him off games and sit him at the wretched piano all day and all night.'

'That's a good idea,' said Soggy malevolently. 'No games, and Mr Crocker can have him for the whole of the games periods. That would please everyone.'

Mr Crocker turned round and glared at Soggy. 'Are you turning my subject into a punishment, Marsh? Are you using it to further this ridiculous, petty nonsense about hair? I protest, Mr Stack!'

'It's a punishment for Pennington already,' Soggy said coldly.

'How dare you!' Mr Crocker had gone bright red,

and his big hooked nostrils distended like a racehorse's. 'Matthews and I are the only people in this school who have got anywhere with Pennington at all, and you are prepared to *use* our successes merely to humiliate the boy over a point of order that is quite meaningless.'

'I agree!' said Matthews. 'Marsh is Pennington's form master, and I admit he has my sympathy in that respect, but the hair thing is his pigeon. You must have known, Marsh, when you gave the ultimatum – you know him well enough, God knows—'

'My hands are completely tied by this soft attitude of the Education Committee. I would—'

'Yes, we all know your natural inclinations,' Crocker said.

'I am afraid corporal punishment for this sort of thing is out,' Mr Stack put in. 'But Pennington must be made to see reason and I do feel – I'm sorry, Matthews, to say this – that the only line of action that stands any hope of succeeding is, as Mr Marsh suggested, through putting him out of all the teams until he toes the line. It will take him out of the limelight, no bad thing – deprive him of his opportunities for showing off. He might well give in.'

'And what if he doesn't? Without him we won't beat Northend Parkside in the gala, and the cup has been ours for three years running!'

'If he's that important, all the more power to the argument,' Mr Stack said. 'I'm sure you will persuade him, Matthews.' He glanced at his watch. 'In any case, he can't swim in the gala like that. He won't be able to see where he's going. I've no more on the agenda. Has anyone else anything to say?'

Penn, released from the Bechstein by the clock striking five, left in mid-bar and made for the Common Room, where Maxwell and the concert party were waiting to start their audition. He met the staff trailing out of the staff room, and was surprised to be waylaid by Matthews at the bottom of the corridor.

'They've passed the buck to me, Pennington. It's either hair and no games, or games and no hair. Think about it.'

He disappeared into the staff gents, leaving Penn seething at the injustice. He shouldered the door into the Common Room and found the concert committee drinking beer, pouring it out of a teapot into innocuous white teacups, with saucers and teaspoons. Looking at the froth, Penn said, 'That wouldn't deceive an infant child.'

Bates was already mellow, he could see. Maxwell said, 'We want you for just about everything, Penn. Midwinter's monologue has to have dirgy stuff for the background, for atmosphere – it's about this grave opening and a corpse getting out. He says it's got music, but he can't find it; but he can sort of tell you how it goes. And the trumpet needs an accompaniment, too. Then Rees and Crombie and Burton are going to do this send-up of the Superbes – they've got the music for that. The sketch is OK, unless you can think of a way of improving it. We've gone over most of the things except Bates's. The girls are using a record for their can-can thing – look, here's the stuff for the Superbes. Let's do that. Have a cup of tea first.'

Penn told them what Matthews had passed on to him, and they were all duly appalled.

'That's stinking, passing it on to Matthews. What are you going to do?'

Penn shrugged. 'Sleep on it,' he said. 'Give Bates another cup of tea,' he added softly. He fetched himself a chair and sat down and while the others argued about what they were going to practise, he played the tune of 'The Red Flag', which was his personal anti-Soggy hate piece, designed to relieve feelings. He played it very loud, hoping it might even reach Soggy out in the corridor.

'Cripes, Penn, you don't half stick your neck out,' Crombie said, grinning.

At Christmas old Crocker had taught the choir to

sing the German carol 'Tannenbaum', which was sung
to the same tune as 'The Red Flag'. It was a popular
choice, being rousing and rhythmic, but Soggy had
objected to its being chosen for the Christmas service
owing to the rebel associations of the tune.

'Highly unsuitable,' he said to Mr Crocker. 'I will
prevail upon Mr Stack to forbid you to use it.'

'It is a carol about a Christmas tree,' Mr Crocker
said, breathing very hard. 'An innocent Christmas tree.
These children are not old enough to know anything
else about it. But if you forbid it, they will find out the
reason why. You have a nasty bigoted mind, and you will
infect these children with your hysterical political views
and make issue where no issue was intended.'

Penn, who had been playing the piano for the choir
and had been sitting near enough to overhear this
exchange, had been intrigued by it, and had played the
tune to his mother at home and asked her what old
Dotty had been talking about.

'It's the tune the Communists used to sing,' his
mother said vaguely. 'In the Revolution and that. I
suppose that's why he doesn't like it. He's a right old
Tory from the look of him.'

This explanation had endeared the tune to Penn. He
liked anything that irritated Soggy. He had played it in
the Common Room the next day when Soggy had

come in to collar Maxwell for a mathematics detention, and Soggy had gone bright red, and come over to the piano, twitching dangerously.

'Why are you playing that tune?' he asked, aware that Penn had heard the exchange of the day before, and suspecting him of pure insolence.

'I'm a Communist, sir,' Penn had replied, playing on.

Soggy had twitched some more, but been uncertain of how to deal with the situation. At the end of the afternoon, when he had had time to think about it, he gave Penn a double detention for some trifling offence, and Mr Stack informed Mr Crocker that 'Tannenbaum' was not to be used in the Christmas service. The whole school knew what had happened, and why the choir's repertoire had been curtailed, and Penn started a Young Communist Party which the whole fifth form joined, although they didn't know a Communist from a Liberal. Ever since, one bar of 'Tannenbaum', whistled or hummed, had the power to send Soggy raving. Only Penn dared to bait him with it and had been caned twice for the pleasure (in spite of the Education Committee).

When he had worked off his feelings Penn obediently went through the bill, working out possibilities. It all seemed very promising. Penn refused point-blank to do a solo. 'You want me to die of overwork? They don't want to hear my stuff, and if I do anything decent old Crocker'll go off the deep end. You know him.'

'Give 'em the old Capritch. It grows on you when you hear it often enough.'

'I haven't noticed,' Penn said coldly. 'Let's get old Bates going. He's nicely away. Bates, stand up. I can't play the ruddy harmonica, thanks to Smeeton – we'll use the piano for now. What do you want, Bates? "Lowlands Away"? "Down by the Royal Albion"?' He played a few exploratory chords. Bates took him up.

'As I was a-walking down by the Royal Albion
The night it was stormy and so was the day,
When who should I see but one of my shipmates
Wrapped up in a blanket and colder than clay.'

Bates's tenor was clear and high, and in sad songs touched a nerve that Penn realized was not peculiar to just himself – so far, Bates's only audience. He sang, when slightly drunk, with such sincerity that the stark words had a pathos that was undeniable.

'His poor head was aching, his sad heart was breaking . . .'

Penn glanced at Maxwell and saw him shut his eyes thoughtfully. Maxwell was held, and even the larking Midwinter. Penn did not play much, merely following with a few suitably poignant chords, feeling it on the harmonica, and cursing Smeeton.

'At the head of the gravestone these words shall be written . . .'

It was perfect, Penn thought, just like in *Mathilda*'s cuddy. He was warm at the thought of being Bates's manager.

When Bates had finished, the audience was impressed.

'Fancy old Bates—!'

'Queer old stuff. Gets you.'

'Yes, but what's eating him exactly?' Crombie said.

'He's dying of VD, you twit,' Penn said.

'Oh, very suitable for a parents' evening,' Maxwell said. 'Just the right touch! That's out for a start. Try something else.'

'They're all earthy,' Penn said.

'We can stand earth, but no subsoil,' Maxwell decided.

Penn guided Bates on to safer ground, with 'Tom's gone to Hilo' and 'Lowlands Away'. When he was well away they did 'The Butcher Boy', and, such was Bates's power, even Maxwell did not question its morality. The difficulty was to stop Bates. Penn was triumphant.

'You're blooming good, Bates. Pipe down now, and stop drinking tea, for cripes' sake. I've got to get you home.'

'The only surefire flop in this old concert,' said Maxwell, 'will be Mr Robert Tate, for whom I am not responsible. The only baritone corpse in the south of England.'

The next day Crocker broke the news to Penn that he was going to have to accompany Mr Tate in the concert, because Mr Tate's usual accompanist was sick.

'Sick of old Tate, I reckon,' Maxwell said.

Crocker said, 'You must come in plenty of time, to go through his songs with him. He says he'll let me know what they are beforehand, but I doubt if he will. I know him. He's not at all considerate, to put it mildly.'

Penn was disgusted to be given a part in the programme the whole school was pledged to despise.

'He's a frightful old woman. Make sure your nails are clean for a change.' Crocker looked worried.

'Suppose *I'm* sick on Saturday?' Penn muttered to Maxwell. 'Sitting there thumping away the whole blooming concert. I was only going to blow the old harmonica for Bates.' He had been doing the Capritch the whole afternoon, while his class went swimming. He hadn't had any time to get his hair cut, even if he had decided to, the rate they were working him. He pointed this out to Matthews, who he could see was getting depressed. In spite of liking Matthews, Penn still hadn't decided what to do. Matthews was entirely sympathetic.

'I might go Saturday morning, then,' Penn said to him, eased by the sympathy.

But on Friday afternoon Soggy, incensed by an insolent remark that Penn had thought he was too far away to hear, gave him a thousand lines to write over the weekend: 'Long-haired boys should learn to keep a civil tongue in their heads.' The punishment was so puerile and so much in keeping with Soggy's arid mentality, that Penn's resolve to go on defying him was renewed.

CHAPTER FIVE

ON SATURDAY MORNING, after writing one hundred and thirty-seven illegible lines, Penn went round to Bates's. The fact that they would have to catch the three o'clock bus back to school for the concert nullified all natural optimism at the thought of a Saturday, and Penn's face was gloomy.

'You coming down to Moorham, till lunch-time?' Penn asked.

'What for?'

Penn shrugged. 'Something to do.'

Bates said, 'You know what you were saying about trying to get some sails for *Mathilda*, so's we could try sailing her?'

'Well?'

'I saw Fletcher this morning and he said there are some smack sails that nobody wants in the old sail loft up Fiddler's Creek. He said Smeeton was going to get them.'

'Did he now?' Penn considered, frowning. *Mathilda's*

sails were in ribbons after their eventful night out, and he had fancied sailing again. He had asked Jim if there were any sails around that anyone didn't want, but Jim couldn't think of any.

'He said they were off old *Bluebell*, and stowed away in the top loft. I was going to come round and tell you.'

'We could go and have a look,' Penn said.

'That's what I thought.'

It would be as less deadly a way to pass the morning as anything else, especially if Smeeton was hanging around up there. They set off, walking, as they both had punctures which they couldn't be bothered to mend. A track led away over Turner's farm, converging with the river. Then it was along the sea-wall, and right-handed into Fiddler's Creek. The old sail loft was derelict, a landmark for some miles around. Once, in the days of barges, the wharf had been busy, but now no one ever came there, except the occasional cranky watercolourist.

Penn wanted to see Smeeton. Smeeton, after the night at sea, had been overheard to say that he would like to kill Penn, but he had made no attempt so far to even annoy him. Penn guessed that he was awaiting his opportunity, which was the way he worked, but Penn's nature was incautious. He was not afraid of Smeeton. He despised him too much.

The tide was just about at its lowest ebb, the creek a

winding snake of mud with a thread of water glistening here and there. They found Fletcher and Gerry Green sitting on the wharf throwing stones at an old can lying in the mud.

Fletcher looked round sourly. 'What you doing down here?'

'Bates said you've found some sails. We thought we'd have a look.'

'Flaming cheek. They're ours if they're any good.'

Penn grinned.

He went round the side of the sail loft with Bates to the rickety old outside ladder that gave access to the top storey. The bottom floor was full of the local farmer's machinery, and the second floor was a mouldering junkheap of old gear off the barges. Penn went up the ladder first, followed by Bates, and then by Fletcher and Gerry. It was steep and rotten, but nothing gave, even under Penn's weight, and he came out at the top on the tiny balcony, some thirty feet high, that gave on to the door. Bates, waiting at the top of the ladder, looked down and said, 'Strewth, Penn, get a move on! This gives me the creeps.' The door was closed by massive oak bars that slotted down into iron brackets. They lifted easily and the door opened inwards. Penn went inside, followed quickly by Bates.

The loft comprised the whole of the top floor,

making a room big enough to lay out a barge mainsail. It was lit by windows overlooking the river and big skylights, so that it seemed almost as if there was no roof at all. The floor was solid, worn smooth by generations of trouser knees, soft slippers and sliding sailcloth. It was also remarkably empty.

'I don't see any sails,' Penn said, lifting an old tarpaulin that seemed to be the only bit of gear around.

It was then, as the door closed, that he got the idea. He stood rigid, not saying anything. It was too late.

'What's up?' Bates said.

The bars dropped in place outside the door with heavy thumps. There was a snigger, and a shuffle, and Fletcher's voice, muffled and distant. 'See you later!'

'I don't get it,' Bates said. 'What's he playing at?'

'Oh, cripes!' said Penn. 'Don't you see?' His face went white momentarily, and a pulse flicked the corner of his mouth. He could not say anything else, choked by pure physical rage. Bates was astonished.

'What's eating you? They're only larking about.' He went over to the door and shoved it. It did not move an inch. 'Fletcher, you idiot!' he bawled.

'Save your breath,' Penn said shortly. He glanced at his watch. It was eleven o'clock. He walked across the room and stood looking down over the empty river. He was so angry at being tricked so easily that he felt almost faint with it, his stomach hollow and sick. The humiliation shook him.

'They'll come back,' Bates said, not very concerned.

'Yes, tonight,' Penn said.

'What do you mean, tonight?'

'After the concert.'

Bates stared at him. 'You don't mean——?'

Penn leaned against the window-frame, picking at the woodworm holes, laying his forehead on the dusty glass. There was a long silence. A swallow flew in through a hole in the top pane and flew out again in a panic with a flurry of wings.

'You mean it's so that you'll miss the concert?' Bates said eventually.

'Smeeton couldn't have found a better way of getting me into trouble if he'd thought for a month.'

'I'm not sorry,' Bates said.

'*You're* not sorry! You're so ruddy chicken, Bates, you make me sick!'

Penn could have wept. He picked at the splintery wood, tearing long strips out of it. He remembered old Crocker telling him to clean his nails. He banged his forehead against the glass, staring down into the shining bed of the creek below. Bates came and stood beside him.

'Perhaps someone might come by,' he said. 'And if we shout——'

'No one comes out here.'

All they could see, thirty feet below, was a stretch of cobbled wharf, quite empty, and the creek. In the far distance, beyond the bluish flat marshes and clumps of old elm, they could see the highest buildings in Northend, some twelve miles away.

'Well, keep looking,' Penn said sourly. 'If you think we're going to have visitors.'

There was certainly no way out. The windows that gave on to the creek were all broken; they could have got out there if there had been a way down. There was also a door in the wall, which opened, but the drop below it was sheer. It had a pulley over the top and had been used to raise and lower goods up and down on a rope. But there wasn't a shred of rope in the loft. The room was painfully bare. Even the tarpaulin was shredding with rot.

'Jump,' said Bates, and shuddered.

Penn opened the door and stood looking down. After a minute or two he looked at his watch again.

'What time's high water today?'

Bates shrugged. 'Around teatime, I think.'

'Five? Half-past four? Yes, it was about midday last Sunday.' Penn leaned against the side of the door, looking down at the wharf below. It was about fifteen feet wide, and very hard, in spite of the grass growing through the cobbles. Beyond it the creek bank sloped away, hard, smooth mud. Penn stroked the scab on his lip, scowling.

'What's up?' Bates said. He wasn't worried.

'Just wondering,' Penn said.

He went on looking. Bates got bored and wandered round the shed, kicking a chip of wood in front of him. 'What'll they do without you, Penn?' he said. 'Old Maxwell will go raving if you don't turn up.'

Penn wasn't bothered about Maxwell. He was going to turn up, because Smeeton thought he wasn't. He hadn't moved his eyes from the wharf.

'When the tide comes up, I'm going to jump,' he said.

Bates stopped kicking his bit of wood.

'You're joking?' he said.

He came and looked out of the hole, pursing up his lips. He looked shaken. 'You don't mean it?'

'When the water's up the wall by about a foot, I reckon there'll be enough to jump into without breaking my ruddy neck.'

'You'll land on the wharf.'

'Not if I take a run at it. There's the whole length of the shed. I reckon I'll land about three feet out from the bank, in about four foot of water. The longer I wait, the better it'll be, but we've got to be in Northend by five, to make it worth the trouble.'

'If high water's half-past four, it won't be up that high much before three.'

'No.'

'You won't catch the bus.'

'We'll bother about that bit when we get to it.'

'You're not really going to, are you, Penn?'

'Yes. I am.'

Penn could be moved by his instinct for revenge to extraordinary daring, as Matthews had noticed several times on the soccer pitch. Now, hate for Smeeton was far stronger than a natural disinclination to attempt the unpleasant exit he was visualizing. Unfortunately, as Penn was not slow to realize, Smeeton was going to get satisfaction of a kind, for the four hours that had to pass before the water came up promised little joy. Sitting in the window, contemplating the distance to the ground for all that length of time was not calculated to cheer.

Bates was no help.

'You'll go splat, as far as I can see,' he said. 'The wharf's too wide.'

Penn glowered. 'If you think I'm going to give Smeeton that much pleasure, you can think again.'

The prospect, of saltings, pasture, cows and the distant haze of the open sea, was serene. The sun poured into the loft and a small breeze chivvied the dust on the floor; a butterfly flew in and sat basking on the window-ledge. Penn lay down in the sun and shut his eyes. He wished it didn't matter . . . for God's sake, he didn't give a hoot about the crummy concert, and would be more than grateful to miss the treat of playing senile accompaniment to that sour-faced mothball, Tate . . . but he was damned if he was going to sit back waiting for Smeeton to come and rescue him, and he was also damned if he was going to let Bates contract out so easily – dozy old Bates, the butt of 5C, who hardly ever uttered in school, treated by all the masters with weary cynicism . . . he had more talent under his spotty hide than any of the rest of Maxwell's line-up. Apart from which, if *he* didn't turn up . . . Penn thought he might as well never turn up again. To go splat in the attempt would be a merciful release compared with the doom which would await him at the Beehive. Penn groaned.

The water started to come back, rippled by the fresh breeze. Penn lay with his chin on his hands, watching it. Far away at the top of the creek two little spots moved on the mud. They were digging for bait, Penn supposed. Pity they hadn't chosen the old wharf. Nothing else human appeared to exist in the world at all. The water was pushing up all the little runnels in the channel, sniffing and withdrawing, and then running up with a

surge, pushing a yellow scum on its lip. It was two
o'clock. Penn shut his eyes again. He should be getting
changed now, scrubbing his fingernails for the baritone
corpse. He picked at them with a nail, and yawned.
Bates was leaning against the far wall, apparently in a
coma.

The tide came up, inexorably as always, and faster,
eventually, than Penn wished. The circus act had very
little appeal, now that it was so close. In spite of Bates's
opinion, Penn did not think there was much risk of
hitting the concrete; it was just that one's natural instinct
was against launching one's all into so much space. Penn
had never been keen on the top board at the best of
times. He stood up, and fidgeted with the woodworm
again. Bates came up beside him and peered down.

'You're not going to, are you?'

'Yes.'

'I don't mind missing the concert a bit.'

Penn thought, When the water covers the wall a foot
– say, up to the bit of seaweed caught on one of the big
stakes – I'll go into orbit. The water came up and
covered it. He took his watch off and gave it to Bates. It
was twenty-five to four. He took off his shirt and
dropped it on the floor.

'Look,' Bates said, 'just for a stupid concert—'

'Oh, belt up.' Penn thought there ought to be a roll

of drums, but all was perfect tranquillity, the skylarks trilling off the wall, the water starting to lap, lap, lap against the wharf, pushed by the summer breeze. He thought of Smeeton's face, and walked back down the shed. The horrid word 'splat' passed through his brain as he started running, and continued with him as he flew through what felt like outer space. But it was water below, not gravestones, and he pulled up his knees to make a shallow landing, grasping them with his hands. The water hit him with a crack, and then it was all completely normal, a mere swim in the creek, his pent-up funk dissolving in a feeling of overwhelming relief. He turned over on his back, kicking against the tide, and waved at Bates's peering face.

'Piece of cake!' he yelled.

He felt more relieved than he would have admitted. He turned over and did a rapid crawl to the bank, smiting the water as if it were Smeeton, savagely triumphant. When he unbolted Bates, Bates looked green.

'I feel sick,' he said.

'Run it off,' Penn said. 'All the way home. We've got to sprint.' He pulled on his shirt, tucking it hastily into his dripping jeans. Bates gave him his watch. It was twenty to four. Half an hour to get home, ten minutes to change . . . it was still a doubtful proposition . . .

barely an hour, and hitchhiking was rotten on a Saturday afternoon. He was starving—

'Come *on!*'

Bates was hopeless.

'What would I have done, if you'd hit the concrete?'

'What would I have done, come to that? I don't see *you* had anything to worry about!'

'I don't know how you could. You've got no imagination, Penn. I feel ghastly.'

Penn said savagely, 'For cripes' sake! It's finished now. Don't be such a girl! Come on—'

He pushed him out, almost kicking him down the ladder. They started to run, but Penn, fit from soccer, went ahead judging the pace to fit the distance. He had to be there long before Bates, for Bates was last on the programme. Bates had all the time in the world. Having estimated thirty minutes Penn got to his garden gate twenty-five minutes after setting off from the sail loft. He vaulted it, squeezed round his father's motorbike which filled the path, and let himself quietly into the kitchen. His mother was out and his father snoring on the bed, for which Penn was profoundly thankful, not wanting to waste time arguing. He changed, combed his damp hair and grabbed the harmonica off his chest of drawers. His father was still snoring. Penn padded downstairs, got himself a hunk of bread and cheese out of the pantry, and let himself out into the garden again. The village street was absolutely deserted, save for the bedraggled figure of an exhausted Bates, weaving wearily up the turning from the farm. It was a quarter past four. Even if he got a lift immediately, he was never going to make it for five. The Beehive wasn't on the main road; there was ten minutes' walk across an estate to get to it. Penn thought of Smeeton, grinning in the audience, and touched the scab on his lip with his tongue. His eyes went to his father's motorbike.

Bates reeled up.

'Come on,' Penn said. 'I've been waiting *hours*—' He opened the gate.

Bates groaned, the sweat trickling down on either side of his nose. Penn heaved the bike off its stand, and wheeled it through the gate. Bates stared.

'Penn, you're not!'

'It'll be all right.' He would get to the concert in time, at least. What might happen afterwards was something to face when the time came. Penn did not believe in looking too far ahead. There was only one thing that mattered just at that moment. He pushed the bike away from the house, and started it up. It was a racing 600cc machine, and the din scorched the village street.

'Get on!' Penn yelled at Bates.

Bates, gibbering with dismay, scrambled on to the pillion.

'What if you meet a copper?' he yelled.

Penn said something very rude that was drowned in the acceleration as he took off down the street. It was a chance he was prepared to take in the heat of the moment. He hadn't sweated all day in that loft to be stopped in the last lap. He took the bend out of the village at forty, and opened up to sixty down the lane. He felt marvellous, completely of the moment, triumphant and fighting. Nobody could do him down. Smeeton would pass out when he arrived.

'Penn, for cripes' sake!' He did not hear Bates moaning, only his frantic hands on his trouser belt. Cripes, if he had a bike of his own—! It was glorious. He cornered on to the arterial, and went into the fast lane, overtaking a Rover 2000 and a Triumph. He didn't care then what happened afterwards: he was in a world of his own, the speedometer passing eighty, and tempted to keep on going. The side road to the Beehive came up like a sick headache. The deceleration depressed his spirits. By the time he got off the bike in the car park he was wondering what the hell had been the point of coming back to deadliness with such fervour. Smeeton had done him a good turn, if he had but recognized it. He could be up there still, watching the butterfly.

Maxwell met him at the door, rolling his eyes. The audience was already dribbling into the hall.

'Old Dotty's raving,' he said. 'He's got a search-party out for you. He's in the music room with the corpse. Hey, what's wrong with old Bates?'

'Nothing's wrong with old Bates,' Penn said. 'Go and find someone to swap clothes with him, and give him a nice cup of tea. With froth on it.'

'I was all right till Penn laid on the transport,' Bates said. He was as white as paper. Penn laughed.

'You won't be laughing when Dotty sees you,' Maxwell said.

Penn shrugged and pushed past, and up the stairs. He must be mad, he thought, seeing the sun coming through the landing window as it had come, warm and lazy, into the loft. That butterfly had more sense. Dotty's face was twitching with rage; he hissed at Penn, 'Are you mad, leaving it as late as this?' The baritone corpse looked him up and down as if he were a freak.

'I would have thought that normal courtesy would have entailed coming in good time,' he said.

Penn said nothing. He had all but broken his neck in the name of normal courtesy, had old Senility had the grace to inquire. Tate was thin, vinegary, with a face like a worn boot. He thought boys should stand to attention when he spoke to them. Penn glowered. Mr Crocker looked at his watch and said, 'We've got twenty minutes. Sit down, Pennington, and Mr Tate will just have time to go through a few points.'

Twenty minutes! Penn thought. The old bike must have shifted. The lettering on the cover of the music was drawn like imitation rustic-work: Penn put it in the first decade of the century.

'I don't suppose you could transpose this into B flat?' Senility said patronizingly.

He was getting his own back. His eyes were nasty, lingering on the abundance of Penn's hair. Penn, hating his guts, transposed into B flat, playing so well that the old windbag was stunned. Crocker, seeing the way Penn was reacting, heaved a private sigh of relief. Tate stood over the piano, and nagged, because Penn wasn't the type of boy he approved of, and Penn didn't listen, ploughing through staves of Victorian codswallop, all trills and frills and melodic swoon. Tate's voice was a drone, like a bluebottle hung up in the net curtains.

'I hope the central heating will be on in the hall, Crocker. It's very sharp for May, and I have to watch my chest. And no smoking. I hope you put a notice up. People have no consideration, no understanding at all. That's marked *dolce*, boy. Use your eyes. And the tempo is too fast. I sing it ter—um, ter—um, ter—um, like that. Keep that left hand softer. Try this one. Start at the bottom of the page. I wonder you can see what you're doing with all that hair. I would have thought Mr Stack would have something to say about these modern tendencies. Can't tell the boys from the girls these days, eh, Crocker? Play the opening bars to this one, keep it flowing . . . it's a sentimental piece, very delicate. And again, do the first six bars again. Yes. When we were young we were proud to look like men. You boys today – God help us all if the country depended on you.' Penn stopped playing and looked at Crocker.

'Yes,' said Crocker hastily. 'I think that's about all we have time for—'

'Fetch me a glass of water,' Tate ordered. 'I must take these tablets before we go down.'

Penn went to get it, and Tate said, 'That boy is an extraordinary pianist, but his manners are non-existent. A typical modern youth. Or teenager, as we are supposed to call them. I really think, if that's the type that is going to run the country in the next few years, the sooner I go to my grave the better.'

Penn came back in time to mutter 'Hear! Hear!' to the last phrase. Crocker gave him a hard, but not entirely unsympathetic, look. While Tate was fussing with his bottle of pills, Crocker said quietly to Penn, 'The old boy's a bit deaf. He won't admit it, but you should know, in case you have to ask him something. Your native mumble will not be understood.'

'Pity the audience isn't deaf, too,' Penn said.

'Yes,' Crocker said, lapsing absent-mindedly from pedagogue to human being. 'He's on the board of governors, you know. We just have to take it, when he offers us his favours.'

Mr Stack and two prefects appeared at the door, smiling and unctuous.

'A very good audience for you, Mr Tate! The hall is quite full.'

They trailed down the stairs, all suiting their pace to Mr Tate's doddering steps. They went on to the stage, behind the velvet curtains, and the noise of the audience could be heard, in leash behind the velvet. Penn knew they were all waiting to leer at the girls' legs, and hear old Finnigan and old Midwinter and old Bates, not deadly old Tate who had to be endured first. He combed his hair; Tate glared at him, and Penn gave him a wide, polite, insolent smile. Maxwell and Crombie were standing in the wings, making messages all over their faces in Penn's direction, and pointing at Bates, who was standing beside them, swaying slightly and staring into space. Maxwell made a cross-eyed drunken face, and did the thumbs up. Penn hoped they weren't overdoing it. Bates's borrowed clothes were slightly bizarre, the blazer being about two sizes too large, and the trousers too short, revealing almost six inches of the unsuitable sky-blue socks he had been wearing with his jeans. Mr Tate was taking another pill, saying to one of the prefects, 'A delicate throat like mine, you can't be too careful this time of year.'

'A tight piece of string would do it the world of good,' Penn murmured.

Mr Stack was stepping forward, making signs to Maxwell to get ready to open the curtains. Mr Crocker and the prefects retreated and Penn sat down at the piano, his face showing nothing but infinite boredom. Mr Crocker turned back and said, 'I'll get you someone to turn the pages.' Penn nodded.

He then saw what was going to happen. He half got up to stop it, but Maxwell was opening the curtains and the full attention of the audience was piling eagerly through the majestically parting velvet, applause and stamping bursting out to relieve the boredom of waiting. The smiling Bates was in Mr Crocker's path, obviously doing nothing – incapable, Penn could see, of doing anything – and Mr Crocker took him by the arm and propelled him gently on the stage. 'Go and turn over for Pennington,' he said. Mr Stack stepped forward to speak, and old Tate cracked his face into affability. Bates wavered out of the wings, and converged, with obvious difficulty, on the piano. He leaned his elbows on the far end of it and gazed at Penn under the lid. 'Fancy seeing you,' he said.

Penn ignored him and opened the first piece of music. Mr Stack was intoning: '. . . so happy today . . . our old friend . . . generously giving his valuable time . . . grateful . . .'

Bates groped his way round the piano's bulk and came and stood beside Penn, breathing heavily. 'I feel sick,' he said. 'But I'll do this little thing for you first.'

Penn looked frantically into the wings, and saw Maxwell and Crombie and Rees and Midwinter all rolling about, doubled up at what had happened. He made furious faces at them, but they just shrugged and made gibbering grimaces, and handclasps over their heads. Penn knew that the idea of livening up Tate's performance appealed to them enormously, and his own predicament was to be all part of the act. He groaned, indignation flooding him. He looked at Bates's green face and whispered, 'Go and get someone else!'

Bates leaned down and put his arm round Penn's shoulders. 'But I want to do it for you, Penn. You're my friend.'

Penn looked at Maxwell, and saw that he was leaning against the wings, helpless with laughter.

'For the first piece, Mr Tate is going to give us . . .'

Tate stood well forward, his back to the piano. Penn glanced down into the audience and saw that their eyes were, as one, on Bates. They were expectant, utterly attentive. He looked at Tate for a signal to start, and saw a little silk tab sticking up over the collar of his jacket, saying: 'Dry-cleaning is recommended for this garment.' He had a neck like a tortoise. Penn played the introduction to 'The Vagabond', Bates wavering over his shoulder, trying to focus on the music. If anyone's jacket, Penn thought, was going to need dry-cleaning . . .

Bates said, 'What's this old crap?'

Penn twitched his shoulder to shake Bates off, but Bates leaned down, still with his arm tenderly round him, and said happily, 'Say when, just say when, and I will tu-urn the page.' His stomach rolled emptily and he said, 'I beg your pardon. I will tu-urn the page whenever you want.'

Penn turned it.

'Hey,' Bates said. 'That's my job. I want to do it for you, Penn. I'm your friend.'

He put his hand out and turned the page while Penn was still at the top of it. Penn flipped it back, snarling, 'Get off me, you creep!'

'Give the jolly heaven above
And the byway nigh me.

Bed in the bush with stars to see,
Bread I dip in the river—
There's the life for a man like me . . .'

'Bread he what?' Bates said. 'Bread he what did
he say?'

'Turn over!'

Bates turned over two pages. Penn, carrying on with
one hand, grabbed at the sheet and shot it back. Bates
leaned over him and with both hands arranged the book,
very deliberately, smoothing it down so that Penn could
only see fragments of what he was supposed to be playing.

'What does he do with his bread?' Bates insisted.

'Move your great mitts, for God's sake!'

Bates turned over again. Penn turned back.

'I'm only trying to help,' Bates said.

Penn could feel the sweat breaking out. Couldn't the
oafs in the wings do something? Obviously not; as one
glance showed him, they were all helpless, holding each
other up.

Bates bent down very earnestly and said in Penn's
ear, 'Did he say he dipped it in the river?'

Penn ignored him.

'That's a ruddy stupid thing to do.'

'Keep your hands off the music!' Penn stopped him
just in time.

'Must be to make it pappy, for his dentures.'

Penn, playing louder to drown Bates's commentary, strained for Tate's bleat. The old vagabond, with his Rolls-Royce parked outside and his central heating and his pep-pills . . . Penn ground his teeth in fury at his lot, holding Bates at bay by playing with his left elbow well out.

When the piece was finished, the applause broke out with astonishing vigour, crashing out of the body of the hall, accompanied by stamping and whistling. Penn saw that the upturned faces were all grinning, full of anticipation. 'Good old Bates!' a voice from the back called out. Everyone clapped again with huge enjoyment. Tate turned round, beaming with pleasure, and said, 'They certainly enjoyed that, didn't they?'

Penn, his hand on Bates's upper arm to stop him bowing, sent a speaking grimace towards Maxwell, appealing for help. But Maxwell was dancing about with his hands clasped over his head, mouthing, 'It's a wow! Keep it up!'

The audience was settling down for a further session, all on the edge of their seats, agog. Stacker, having taken a seat in the front row after making the introduction, had his eyes on the piano, glazed. His whole body was stiff. The sight of him, obviously prepared, like Penn himself, for disaster, gave

Penn the feeling that judgement day was not far off.

Tate was wavering: '. . . that lovely old ballad . . . one of the heritages of our glorious . . .' Penn fingered the music. What lousy old ballad, for heaven's sake, out of the mildewed pile in front of him? Bates had one foot up on the piano stool, doing up his shoelace.

'These socks are all wrong for this sort of thing,' he said. 'They're sports socks. Not formal socks.'

'"Cherry Ripe",' said Tate.

Everyone cheered and clapped. Penn winced.

'The old cherries,' Bates said. 'They're underneath "Annie Laurie". I saw them. Squashed flat by now.'

Penn flipped up the right sheet, very tattered, all trills and pencil marks.

'Ripe, I'll say it's ripe,' Bates said. 'You know, Penn, when you passed that Rover on the arterial, if he took your number, you'll be in jug. There's a fifty limit on that stretch.'

Penn, just about to start, dropped his hands and hissed at Bates, 'Get off this stage, you drunken basket!'

Tate turned round, his bonhomie frozen on his face, and met Penn's eyes, incredulous. Penn took a deep breath, switched his gaze to the music and plunged into a startled introduction, drowning in the scurry of ornamentation, concentrating hard. Tate came in two bars late, still gasping, and Penn braked, finding him. Bates turned over.

Penn let out a yelp.

'Say when,' Bates said. 'I'm ready for you.'

'Leave it alone!'

'Cherry ripe, cherry ripe,
Ripe, I—I cry—y . . .'

'Cherry tripe, cherry tripe,' Bates intoned. 'Triipe, I cry.' He hiccupped and said, 'These old cherries give me the pip.' He laughed. Penn snorted, seeing the big hands swoop like owls in daylight over the music rack. He knocked one up out of the way, and went on playing with one hand, fending Bates off. Bates struggled with him and Penn brought his elbow up and jabbed him sharply in the stomach. Bates let out a groan, and Penn withdrew abruptly, remembering . . .

'All right, now!' he spat at Bates.

Bates turned with such vigour that the frail sheets came apart and started to slide in a shower down over the keys and on to the floor, followed in a slippery, musty-smelling stream by 'Annie Laurie', 'The Rose of Tralee', 'Barbara Allen' – '"And Uncle Tom Cobbleigh and all",' Bates said loudly, dropping down on his hands and knees. Penn swept all the paper aside, shut his eyes, and improvised, going down fast. Bates was underneath the piano, lumbering about on his hands and knees. 'Cripes, Penn, I do feel ill,' he said at knee-level.

'We're nearly there,' Penn muttered. 'Hold it, for God's sake.'

He was clammy and shaking, and did not know the tune after 'Where my Julia's lips do smile', so went straight back to the chorus, losing Tate *en route*. That was his bad luck. Bates put his hand on the pedal and Penn trod on it. Tate caught up. Bates started to retch quietly to himself. Penn brought the melody to an abrupt close, got up from the piano stool, marched over to the curtain pulley and pulled hard. The audience broke into a thunderous roar of clapping, cheering, and whistling so rapturous that Tate, pop-eyed with rage at Penn's eccentricity, was forced to change his mind. He stepped forward, smiling, and disappeared from view in a swoosh of velvet and dust.

Penn leaned against the wings, overcome by the experience. He felt like sobbing. The others went to fetch Bates, so weak with laughter that they looked as drunk as he did. Behind the curtain the audience was roaring.

'You've ruined it, Pennington,' Maxwell was moaning. 'It was ruddy marvellous, and you've finished it. Listen to them!'

The audience was shouting, 'Bates! Bates! Good old Bates!' Maxwell opened the curtains again and revealed Mr Tate still bowing, coughing slightly, but wreathed in smiles. Penn went back to the piano, gathered up the music and sat down. Tate came over to him, overcome by the enthusiasm.

'How they love a good old song! Just hark at them!'

Penn looked at Stacker, and saw that he was running a finger round his neck, just inside his collar. He looked back at Penn and inclined his head slightly, once or twice. Very ominously.

'You can take a bow. Just one,' said Tate.

Penn got up and bowed to Mr Stack. The audience roared again. Penn sat down.

'"Pale Hands I Love",' Tate said to Penn.

Oh, God, thought Penn. To think, he could still have been lying in the loft, with the butterfly.

CHAPTER SIX

IN THE INTERVAL Penn went to Maxwell and said, 'Where's Bates? What've you done with him?'

'We can't do anything with him, that's the trouble. You'd better see him,' Maxwell said. 'He's laid out.'

Bates was in the Common Room, moaning, his head in his hands.

'What did you give him, for heaven's sake?' Penn muttered to Maxwell. 'He only needed——' He looked at Bates in despair. The day's adventures had done for Bates. Penn, with ten minutes to get results, took charge.

'Find him something to eat. He's starving. Then a nip of the First Aid brandy just before he goes on. That should do it.'

'How are you going to get the First Aid brandy, for Pete's sake?'

'I know where the key is,' Penn said.

'You'll get killed if anyone sees you.'

'You go and get him something out of the dining-room. Buck up!'

Bates said, 'I'm not going to do it, Penn. They were laughing at me just now, and I was only turning pages. What if I get up and sing—'

'Oh, stow it. I'll be doing it with you, won't I? You know the stuff backwards.'

Bates sobbed.

'Oh, you're such a crawling twit, Bates!' Penn breathed.

There was very little time. He sprinted up to the staff room, head down. The corridor was empty. He knocked at the door and, to his relief, there was no answer. He went in, took the appropriate key off its hook on the keyboard, and unlocked the petty cash drawer in Soggy's desk. The flask of brandy was at the back, underneath the paperwork. He pulled it out. It only needs Soggy, he thought, to walk in now . . . He heard the door handle rattle, and aged ten years. Maxwell put his head round.

'Got it?'

Penn leaned against the lockers, shivering.

'It's me that needs it now,' he complained bitterly. 'Bates can't feel anything like as bad as I do, after what's happened.'

'Stacker wants to see you afterwards. He's sent someone round already so you get the message loud and clear.'

'Well, I did my best, didn't I? What else could I've done?' Stung by the bitter injustice, Penn galloped back to the Common Room. Crombie and Rees were stuffing Bates with chocolate éclairs. Bates was too weak to protest. Penn took the top off the brandy and took a few swallows. Someone was shouting for him from the wings.

'You've got to go on. It's Midwinter's monologue.' Maxwell gave him a shove.

Penn gave him the brandy bottle. 'Look, about five swallows'll do him. Time it properly.' He leaned over Bates and said, 'You can do it. You're great, Bates. You show 'em. I'll come back for you in a minute. Don't you worry.'

It was while he was playing the dirge music for Midwinter, which was the same notes nearly all the time, so that he had almost gone into a coma, that he saw a face in the audience that almost stopped him in mid-chord. It was his bird, the folk-song girl. She was in the third row, smiling, her hair hanging in whitish, shining wings down over her leather jacket. Penn felt as weak as Bates, staring, his heart pounding, all the blood rushing up into his neck. He looked away, trying to breathe slowly, trying to pretend it didn't matter. But it mattered terribly. When he came to stand up at the end he felt as if he were an elephant, engulfing the stage.

He went back to Bates, slowly, and sat down. He lay back in the old cane chair, looked at the ceiling, and took long calming breaths. Maxwell came in and said, 'What's eating you? You're on after the next.' Penn thought, I must talk to her afterwards. Find out where she lives.

'Yes,' he said.

I never knew it could get you like this, he thought.

'Shall I dose Bates?'

'Yes.'

Ten minutes later he was standing in the wings with Bates, waiting for the girls' can-can to finish. Maxwell was looking at them dubiously. Bates was still white, looking distant, glazed and zombie-ish, and Penn was strangely subdued, as if all the fight had gone out of him. He looked nervous. Maxwell had never seen Penn nervous in the whole course of his career. Having stolen the First Aid brandy and chucked the empty bottle in the dustbin in the kitchen would have been good reason – for anyone else – to look worried, but Maxwell knew that Penn took such incidents in his stride. Whatever was on his mind, it wasn't that. Maxwell got ready to close the curtains, recognizing his cue in the Offenbach record. So far the concert had been a wow. Maxwell sent up a brief prayer for the last item to be as good as the first. At least it had the same leading man.

After the row had calmed down, Penn went on to the stage, marching Bates in front of him with a hand firmly on his elbow. He thought that Bates was in the right mood, with an otherwhereness glaze in his eyes, but he wasn't sure that he might not, if the worst came to the worst, pass out altogether. Penn, taking care not to look into the audience, blew a few runs on the harmonica and launched straight into 'Lowlands Away'. They could hardly make a greater hash of the thing than they had, between them, in the first item.

Bates nearly didn't start. Penn could see him shrinking, the panic in his eyes. He played softly, willing Bates, watching him, playing the melody twice over until the moment came when Bates either had to go or retire altogether. Penn saw his mouth open. Penn shut his eyes, and drew on the sonorous D that started the verse, willing Bates with such energy that it was as if the voice came without Bates having anything to do with it.

'I dreamed a dream the other night . . .'

Penn was so relieved that his breath shook, the melody quavering. But Bates, once away, like a body of water released from a dam, started to flow as if there had never been a doubt at all, his voice in perfect control.

Penn saw his expression change, relax, and the look come into his eyes that meant he was in charge. Penn could leave him, ornamenting, playing a weaving harmony high above Bates with his mind free to concentrate, the awful doom he had been anticipating put away. The scab on his lip was a curse, getting hung up occasionally with fearful pricks, but Penn remembered that he had beaten Smeeton yet again, and the sad tune went soaring and Bates was with him: they would show the lot of them what a real song was . . . Penn was happy.

The applause for 'Lowlands Away' was long, astonished, and genuine. The school had never known old Bates could do it.

'You've got to give 'em something cheerful before "The Butcher Boy",' Penn said to him urgently. 'You can't give 'em all morgue stuff.'

'"Down by the Royal Albion",' Bates said.

'Over my dead body,' Penn said.

He started on 'The Golden Vanity', which had a corpse, but a merry tune to go with it. Bates muttered something at him and did not come in, so Penn came round again, needling Bates with such a stern eye that he took off in the right place, and never looked back. Penn was breathless by the end.

Bates had no inhibitions now about singing the tale

of the wronged maid. The others had been mere throat-clearing. His voice was full of self-pity, soft, and yet clear to the back of the hall. It had the direct quality that Penn could not put words to, a lack of affectation that put the story across so vividly that Penn could feel the involvement of the audience like a tangible link reaching out over Maxwell's footlights. Bates believed each word of it and his voice as an instrument carried every nuance as plainly and as perfectly as the story demanded.

'Oh, dig my grave long, wide and deep,
Put a marble stone at my head and feet,
And in the middle a turtle-dove
That the world might know that I died for love.'

It faded, and Penn faded with it, and the shades of Mr Tate were buried, defeated utterly by a plain skill that the old man had professed and never possessed all his singing days. There was a silence that Penn recognized as the greatest compliment accorded during the whole of the show; then the audience broke out into a roar of appreciation that made Bates look at Penn in amazement.

'Bow,' said Penn. 'Go on. Do the thing properly.'
Bates grinned. Penn laughed.

Maxwell closed the curtains. They were all rushing about and capering, the tension broken in the lovely sound of the audience all with them, and cheering like mad. Bates had to go out again and bow. Everybody clapped and stamped. Mr Stack stood up and made the usual blah, and then the audience was filing out, making for the spread laid out in the dining-room. Penn went to the exit nearest to where his bird had been sitting, and Bates followed him as a matter of habit. They stood in the corridor outside the door, Penn craning for a glimpse of the blonde hair.

'Let's go and get something to eat,' Bates said. 'Who are you looking for?'

'That girl who sang in the hall at Moorham was here. I saw her. I want to talk to her.'

'What on earth for?'

They were pushed all ways. Penn didn't know what he was going to say anyway, only that he had to make the effort, or suffer for it. When he saw her he felt all the blood rushing again, and the embarrassment like a suffocation. He was speechless. Bates gave him a shove. Penn stared, his shoulder braced against the pushing throng. The girl turned, saw Bates, and stepped out of the crush against the wall and said, 'I think you were marvellous.'

Bates gave her an idiotic grin and nudged Penn.

Penn could have strangled him. He couldn't think of anything to say, and went on staring, and the girl said to Bates, 'I've never heard that song before. I've never heard you before either. Do you sing with any of the clubs?'

Bates looked at Penn to see what was silencing him. Penn, with the effort it might have cost him to push a steamroller into motion, said, 'Can we take you down to tea? We heard you sing at Moorham one night, a week or two back, and we thought you were pretty good, too.'

It was the greatest social breakthrough of his career.

The girl gave him a dazzling smile and said, 'Oh, thank you, yes,' and dropped her long black eye-lashes in a way that made Penn's toes curl up.

'Pennington.'

The voice behind him was unmistakable. Most of the crowd had gone now, and they had tagged on to the last stragglers tailing down the corridor. Penn turned round just as Soggy drummed a fore-finger on his shoulder.

'Mr Stack wants you in his room, immediately.'

'Sir, I—'

'Go!'

Penn hesitated. Soggy's hand closed round the back of his neck and propelled him bodily across the corridor and through the archway back into the hall. Penn wrenched himself free and turned on Soggy with a look on his face that made the teacher take an involuntary step backwards. Penn saw the malice in Soggy's eyes, and knew that he had treated him like that, in front of the girl, with a perfect awareness of what it meant. It was not blundering tactlessness; it was intended, and enjoyed. Penn thought for a second that he was not going to be able to stop himself from hitting him, but the habit of the infinite deadly number of his years at school proved effective. He was able to control himself; he closed up, shutting his face, hunching his shoulders, pushing his hands into his pockets. He stared at Soggy, and Soggy looked at him and said, 'You insolent young beggar.'

Penn went and knocked at Stacker's door. When he went in, Mitchell was standing looking out the window.

'The police constable wants a word with you, Pennington,' Stacker said. 'It's about a motorbike.'

In that instant several points registered in Penn's mind. He knew that his face had – momentarily – betrayed alarm at the mention of the word 'motorbike', and that Mitchell had seen it. Mitchell had been watching for it. But Mitchell's own face also betrayed rage at Stacker's slip in giving away the object of the interview. Penn, used to police procedure, recognized immediately the advantage Stacker had inadvertently given him. He did not say anything. He realized that he was in an extremely precarious situation.

'I've no doubt,' Stacker said – obviously having a great deal – 'that you will be able to clear up whatever it is the constable wants to know. Meanwhile I must go down and play the host, Mitchell, if you will excuse me.'

He bowed himself out and Mitchell perched himself on the desk and said to Penn, 'Sit down.'

Penn was thinking furiously behind a truculent expression. He knew perfectly well that riding his father's bike without permission and without a certificate of insurance was an arrestable offence. Oakhall was just around the corner, unless some miracle happened. This was it, the moment he had least expected it. He waited, silent, watching Mitchell getting ready to pat him about, a cat with a mouse. He felt resigned and sick and hating Mitchell so much that he could scarcely bear to look at him. He had been expecting a domestic row about manners and alcohol, not this. He was tired, and now he was going to have to think like blazes.

But Mitchell was unexpectedly inexact in explaining his mission.

'I just want to know what you've been doing today. Where you went. Times, if you know them. Anyone who saw you.'

Penn hesitated. He knew that he was within his

rights to keep quiet, but he doubted whether such outright uncooperation would improve his case. To answer wasn't difficult, but the story was unusual. Too unusual, Penn hoped, for Mitchell to feel he was making it up. Mitchell knew the sail loft. When Penn said he had jumped out, Mitchell looked at him narrowly. He took notes of everything Penn said. Penn did not hurry, saying as little as possible, so that Mitchell had to prompt him a good deal.

'What time did you jump out?'

Penn wanted to make it earlier, so that he could give himself more leeway when it came to the time it had taken him to travel to Northend, but the time was tied to the height of the water in the creek, which could be checked. He couldn't say he jumped into a dry creek: he wouldn't be there to tell the tale. He dragged it out, saying he hadn't really noticed.

'You could show me, if we were on the spot, how high the water was when you jumped? You must have been very careful about this, surely?'

'Yes.'

'You jumped as soon as you thought it safe?'

'Yes.'

'How high is the loft?'

'About thirty feet, I suppose.'

'Risky, wasn't it?'

Penn shrugged.

'Anyone see you?'

'Only Bates.'

'Was that the boy who sang?'

So Mitchell had been in the audience, Penn noted. If Mitchell asked Bates anything, Penn knew he was doomed. Bates was a hopeless liar. Penn couldn't understand why Mitchell was bothered about the loft episode.

'What did you do when you were out?'

'Unlocked Bates. Went home.'

'Straight home?'

'Yes.'

'Anyone see you?'

'No.'

'Anyone at home? Anyone who could say what time you got in?'

Penn could feel his mouth getting dry. He could see Mitchell watching for exactly such symptoms.

'My father was in.'

'What then?'

'I changed and came here.'

'How?'

'My father ran me in on his motorbike.'

It was a gamble. Penn could feel the sweat breaking out. He was so flaming guilty he felt as if the word was stuck in writing all over him, like the message on the Major's Jaguar.

Mitchell sat up and read through his notes, tapping his pencil against his teeth.

'Can you ride a motorbike?' he asked.

'Yes.'

'Got a licence?'

'No.'

Penn sat very still. He could feel a bead of perspiration on his lip, and dared not wipe it away. He thought Mitchell could see it. Mitchell was looking at the notes, pursing his mouth, thoughtful.

'I'd like to see Bates,' he said. 'Where will he be? Still here?'

This time Penn knew his face gave him away. He opened his mouth and stumbled on the first word. He cleared his throat.

'In the dining-room,' he muttered.

Mitchell went to the door and out across the corridor to the staircase, where he bellowed for a boy who was on the stairs at the bottom. He gave his message and came back, knowing perfectly well that Penn had considered flight, and seen the uselessness of it. He sat on the desk again and watched Penn, and Penn looked at the floor.

'Your headmaster not say anything about your

hair?' he said, after a long silence.

Penn did not reply.

Mitchell repeated his question.

'What's it got to do with it?' Penn's voice quivered.

'To do with what?' Mitchell said.

Penn was silent. He knew Mitchell was trying to break him, and he knew Mitchell was damned nearly succeeding.

'Do the girls like it?'

'I haven't asked them.'

'What's it for, then?'

'To keep me warm.'

Mitchell's eyes narrowed again.

'What did you do to your lip?'

'I cut it.'

'How?'

'Talking.'

Mitchell said, 'You're asking for it, Pennington, aren't you?'

There was another long silence, relieved eventually by the hesitant entry of Bates. He saw Penn sitting in the chair, and Mitchell on the desk, and his mouth opened.

Mitchell said, 'What time did Pennington jump out of the loft?'

Bates blinked, and said, 'Twenty to four. Why?'

Penn looked at Mitchell and saw the shock of surprise carefully covered up. He felt a stab of satisfaction.

'Why are you so sure of the time?'

'Penn gave me his watch to hold.'

Mitchell nodded, and wrote. Penn felt that Bates had thrown him, but could not understand the way the interview was going any more. He felt as if the pressure was off him, but Mitchell was still there, and the motorbike was still down in the yard, if Mitchell chose to go and look. He did not move, avoiding looking at Bates. Bates was more dangerous than anything. Penn thought of the silver-haired girl and shivered.

Mitchell said to Bates, 'All right. You can buzz off.'

Bates did so, with an alacrity that twisted Penn. Mitchell stood up and said, 'Come and see me tomorrow. At the station. Say three-thirty.'

'Is that all?'

'For now.'

Penn was amazed. He got up and went out of the room and downstairs and into the bog, while Mitchell got clear. Then he went out into the yard, and watched Mitchell get into his white police Mini and drive away. He went out of the main gate and towards the town centre, not stopping to look for a motorbike on the way. Unless he had already seen it. Penn, very puzzled, went out and found the machine exactly as he had left it, behind the bike shed. He stood fingering his lip. He felt he ought to feel relieved, but he had a feeling that Mitchell was preparing a trap for him. He felt unsure of what Mitchell was getting at, wondering whether his own guilt had made him jump to conclusions when Stacker said it was about a motorbike. Mitchell's questions had not fitted in with what Penn thought it was all about; just as they had come to the hot spot, Mitchell had lost interest.

Penn looked at the bike. The yard was completely empty. It was going dusk, and the supper party was in full swing away on the other side of the school. Penn knew that to ride home on the bike was risky, but to leave it behind was impossible. There was his father to face, besides the police. And the sooner he got home and told his father about the lie that he must substantiate if Mitchell chose to check up on it – and Penn knew that Mitchell would – the safer he would be. There was no doubt in Penn's mind that his father would stick up for him before the police; there was also little doubt that telling his father what he had done was not going to be funny.

But his father knew. Penn didn't have to say anything, only screw up enough courage to step into the kitchen, and it all broke round him, almost literally. His father had heard the bike, and came in from the television, his face distorted with his wild temper. His wife came with him, saying frantically, before anything happened, 'Leave him alone, Bill, for God's sake!'

'I'll leave him alone when I've finished with him — it won't take long!'

Penn put his arms up over his face and half turned, hunching a shoulder, ducking his head. He would have been all right, save in the ensuing fracas, ducking neatly sideways to avoid one of his father's wilder blows, he came up sharply against the hard metal of the tin-opener fixed to the wall and nearly knocked himself out. As he went down he saw his mother pick up a frying-pan and swing it like a golf club. It glanced off his father's shoulder and went straight into a row of glass jars full of sugar, rice and currants. Penn hit the floor and doubled up, like a jockey under Becher's, rice, sugar, and currants falling like rain. His father kicked him, twice, before his mother went at him again, and Penn heard their voices, rising and falling in torrents of blame and hate while they grappled, and — far away in the dark front room — the noise of Mrs Jones's poker hammering on the wall.

Penn dragged himself into a sitting position, resting his head against the gas cooker. His father was puffing like a grampus; Penn knew the way of it, and listened to the invective that flowed over him, rich and familiar and inventive, so that he was almost able to admire it. The tin-opener had caught him just over the eyebrow. He felt dizzy, and starving hungry. His mother was crying.

Then Penn realized that Mrs Jones's poker had turned into something much nearer at hand.

'Go to hell!' his father roared.

Penn staggered to his feet, urgent and scared.

'Dad, listen! It's the police—'

His father was silent, instantly. 'What have you done?' he whispered to Penn. 'Is it the bike?'

'I said you drove me in. We left about a quarter past four.'

'What, and back?'

'I suppose so. He didn't ask. He just asked about how I got to school.'

'You—' His father swore at him. The knock came again, loud and authoritative. 'Why should I get you off, you little—' His father went off again, his words foul.

'Get on with it, you fool,' his wife chocked at him.

He went out into the hall at last, shutting the door behind him.

Penn leaned against the wall, very tired and sore, but not frightened. He got out his comb and started to put his hair to rights. The voices argued at the front door, and Penn knew that there was no immediate cause for alarm.

Thank God, he thought, for a father you can trust.

'Two blokes went out to Fiddler's Creek on a motorbike, left it by the sea-wall and went out on to the mud to dig for bait. At two o'clock, as near as we can fix it, they heard someone start it up and drive it away. By the time they got up on to the wall to see, it had vanished. It was found, two hours later, abandoned and pretty well smashed up, on the outskirts of Northend. Patrick Pennington by his own admission, was up at Fiddler's Creek at two o'clock. He and his friend John Bates were seen going up there by Turner's tractor-man at ten o'clock. They did not come back while the tractor-man was working, which was until two o'clock.' Mitchell mumbled away, leafing over his notes, while Sergeant West was locking up for the night.

'And what is Pennington's alibi? I've no doubt he's got a very good one?' West asked.

'Yes, he has.' Mitchell outlined it. West's eyebrows went up at the mention of the jump out of the sail loft.

'That's hard to take. I'd like to see him do that.'

'Yes. That's what I thought. I'm going to take him up there tomorrow and see if he sticks to the story. I'm pretty sure I'll get him, because he's frightened about something. When the word motorbike came up, he nearly jumped out of his skin. Just for a moment. And

153

he was worried when I was questioning him. Very worried.'

'He didn't say much, if I know him.'

'Minimum. What he did say, apart from yes and no, was insolent.'

West sighed. 'I thought we might be getting somewhere with him. But with parents like he's got – what can you expect? It might not be a bad thing if he's sent away for a few months.'

'I gather that his headmaster wouldn't be sorry to see it happen. He says they can't do anything with him.'

'It's not for lack of wits. Just bloodymindedness,' West said. 'Bad example at home, no one to guide him. Even the probation officer's had enough. He says you might as well talk to a sack of potatoes. The parents never stop hammering the lad at home, but as soon as we suggest that his behaviour isn't all it might be, they do a right-about turn and make out that the boy is God's own gift to the universe. What can you do?'

'I can't work up much sympathy for him, I'm afraid.' Mitchell put his file away and locked the drawer. 'Funny thing,' he added. 'A yob like that being musical. I got stuck with watching the last half of their concert. He can play the piano as if he's not even thinking about it.'

'Probably isn't. Thinking is the one thing that comes hard to Pennington.'

'I shall be surprised if we don't get him on this.' Mitchell sounded satisfied, as West put out the lights. 'I'll swear he's lying somewhere along the line. The business about the loft — if that's the truth, I'm a Dutchman.'

CHAPTER SEVEN

BY THE TIME Penn went up to Bates's the next morning, he knew what Mitchell was after. His father, having repaired to the pub for refreshment after beating up his family, learned about the theft of the motorbike from the top of Fiddler's Creek. He went home and woke Penn up, threatening him drunkenly and loudly, until Mrs Jones pounded her shoe against the wall. But Penn knew he was in the clear, and slept more soundly after his father's visit. Everything was explained. If he was lucky, he would get out of the tangle without his own actual crime being discovered. But Bates had to be fixed.

'If he asks you how you got to school yesterday, you've got to say you hitchhiked,' Penn told Bates. 'I told him my father drove me there and back on the bike, and my father's told him the same. But if you go and say it was you on the pillion, for heaven's sake, he'll know something's up.'

'All right,' Bates said, not very eagerly.

'Say someone picked you up and took you all the way, someone you've never set eyes on before. Don't be clever and say it was Miss Marble or somebody, else he'll check up and prove you're a liar. Say a fawn Anglia, or something, nothing conspicuous.'

'All right.'

'He probably won't bother. It's earlier on he's trying to work out. And we're cast-iron in the clear for that, thanks to Fletcher.'

Business over, Penn hesitated before he opened the subject that was as much on his mind as the motorbike escapade. Trying to sound as if it was just something to say, to fill in the silence, he mumbled, 'You find out that bird's name yesterday?'

'What bird?'

'The one you took down to tea, when Soggy butted in.'

'Oh, her. Yes.'

'What is it?'

'Sylvia.'

'Where does she live?'

'How should I know?'

Penn shut his eyes, strangling inclinations towards violence. A deep, bitter disappointment pulled him down. He could not keep it out of his voice.

'Cripes, Bates, you knew! You could have asked——!'

'What do we want to know for?' Bates asked indignantly. 'I got landed with buying her a cup of tea, didn't I? What else was I supposed to do? Ask her round to supper?'

'Didn't you find anything out? What she does? What club she sings with or something?'

'Oh, yes, she did natter on. Oh, yes. She invited me round to sing at the place she goes to. What do you think of that?' Bates giggled.

'What did you say?' Penn breathed.

'Not on your nelly.'

'Where is it, this place?' Penn was so patient it was making him shiver.

'It's called the Old Barge Club. Meets on a barge. In Northend somewhere – the gasworks jetty, I think. She said there's going to be a Folk Festival and they're going – it's in Tolchester next month. Would I like to go and sing "The Butcher Boy"? With my friend. That's you, Penn. It's on the nineteenth of June. There you are. What more do you want?'

Penn started picking bits of moquette out of Mrs Bates's chair arm, where the cat had pulled them. The nineteenth of June was the date of the Andante and Rondo Capriccioso.

'Pat, stop wrecking my furniture! Clear out into the kitchen. I've got my work to do.' Mrs Bates gave him a shove with her dustpan. 'When are you going to get your hair cut, if it's not a rude question? They think our John's courting, seeing you around.' She laughed.

Penn scowled at her.

'Cheer up, love. It might never happen.' Mrs Bates was a lot nicer than his own mother.

'It has,' he said.

'You look like it,' she said happily.

They mooched out into the kitchen. Penn told Bates about the nineteeth of June. Bates said, 'That lets us out nicely, then. I couldn't go without you.'

'We'll go,' Penn said.

'But you can't.'

'Why can't I? There's no law I've got to play in the Northend thing, is there? It's a Saturday. Even Crocker can't force me.'

'But, Penn, what'll he say? He'll go raving. All that work you're putting in.'

'Good reason for packing it in. We'll go to this thing in Tolchester. He can say what he likes.'

The girl's face, inviting Bates, smiling at him, scoured Penn. 'We'll go to the Old Barge and you can sing. You're better than any of 'em, Bates.'

'It's just the girl you're after.'

Penn didn't say anything, thinking of her so close yesterday, and her eyes with that stuff making them look enormous, and her hair, and then Soggy talking to him like that in front of her, and putting his hand on the back of his neck and shoving him, as if he was two years old. Penn could feel the blood coming up into his face at the memory of it, and his feeling towards Soggy was so wild he was almost frightened of it. He thought he could kill him quite easily. He would enjoy it.

In the afternoon he went down to Moorham to meet Mitchell. He wasn't as worried as he had been yesterday, but he knew he had to be very careful. He could see that Mitchell had good reason for believing that he had pinched the bike, and the possibility that he might be booked for something he hadn't actually done was unnerving.

Mitchell had a Northend copper with him, another sharp-eyed youngish bloke. They told him to get in the back of the car, and drove him out to Fiddler's Creek. Mitchell parked the car on the quay, and they stood there contemplating the wharf, and the door in the sail loft high above. It was a grey day with a fresh breeze blowing in from the sea. The water was scuffled with waves, lapping up over the mud.

'If you jumped in at twenty to four yesterday, you could do it today at twenty to five, allowing roughly an hour for the advance of high water. We want to get these times right. You jumped as soon as you thought you could get away with it?'

'Yes.'

Penn knew he was safe with his times. The tide, give or take ten minutes, was not going to play him up, unless the end of the world was at hand. The two coppers made him take them up into the sail loft, where they opened the door that gave out over the creek and stood looking down.

'This is where you jumped from?'

'Yes.'

'You don't want to change your mind about this story?'

'No.'

Penn, looking out, too, was not surprised at Mitchell's scepticism. In the cold grey wind the prospect looked, somehow, far nastier than it had looked the day before. The ground looked much farther away, and harder, the white Mini very small below; even the water looked dangerous. He began to feel worried. Mitchell glanced at his watch.

'Four-fifteen.'

There was still mud below. Penn leaned against the wall, trying not to think of anything. He supposed Mitchell would wait till the water came up high enough, check on the time, and then they would clear off. There was nothing he could get him on. He kept thinking about the girl. Sylvia. He couldn't think of her as Sylvia, somehow.

At twenty to five the water was a good foot short of where it had been when he had jumped. Mitchell looked at it and said, 'I don't believe your story, Pennington. Anything more you'd like to say?'

Penn was outraged.

'How else did we get out, then? You see if you can open that other door when the bars are down!'

'I'm just suggesting that you tell the truth now, before it's too late.'

'I have told you the truth.'

'All along the line?'

Penn's eyes flicked. 'Yes.'

'I don't believe you. I'm warning you now, anything you say may be taken down and used—'

Penn felt the flames rise. 'You ruddy coppers! You believe just what you want to! I'll show you I did it, if you don't believe me!'

Mitchell laughed.

Penn straightened up, and moved very fast. He saw the expression change on Mitchell's face very abruptly. He knew the wind was blowing off the marshes, into the sail loft, and he was short of a valuable foot of water and that, this time, the circus act was extremely dangerous, but it did not stop him. It was as good a way to go under as any, and take Mitchell with him, come to that. 'Lad questioned by police throws himself to death.' Penn threw himself. The death part was an eyelash away. The fear, falling, was terrible. The wind held him back, and it was only the edge of the water below, and the big stakes and the roof of the Mini – all to stop Mitchell's scorn. Penn would have embraced Mitchell now, if there was any way Mitchell could have stopped him. He curled up and got his head down between his forearms, and the name Sylvia ran right through him, like electricity. He hit two feet of water and the bed of mud, and his ankles took the shock, and his soccer knee screamed out, but he wasn't dead. A tiny, awkward sliver of him was disappointed.

Floundering, he launched himself forward into the balm of deep water, and let it hold him while he took stock. He had no breath and coherent thought beyond amazement that he was still alive. The two policemen were staring down. Penn swam to the old jetty downstream, against the tide, wondering which of the pains were going to meet him when he got out. He was going to get out and walk away, even if it killed him. He saw that he still had his watch on and was furious. He'd send the repair bill to Mitchell.

He got out, trying to look as if he was in no hurry,

because he couldn't hurry. Besides his knee, which didn't want to hold him, he was flabby with shock. But he climbed the wall, holding on to the jetty, and stood up at the top, pushing his hair back. The wind was cold and went right through him. He saw Mitchell and his colleague come out of the shed on to the top of the ladder, so he turned his back, shoved his hands in his pockets and started to walk home along the sea-wall, willing his knee to bear up. He didn't turn round, but he heard the Mini start up and drive away towards the top end of the creek.

It was a very long way home.

His father thought the story a huge joke and laughed like mad.

'That's the way to show the beggars!' he kept saying. He got Penn some dry clothes, and rubbed his knee with wintergreen. He poured out two cans of beer, and held one up to Penn, who lay back in the armchair and turned on the television.

'Here's to us,' he said. 'Disaster to all coppers.'

Penn smiled.

'There's a load of us saw you drive in on that motorbike,' Smeeton said to Penn. 'If any old copper starts asking, that is.'

'What did the copper want?' Crombie asked.

'He wanted to congratulate me on my performance in the concert,' Penn said.

They laughed derisively. They shouted at each other, the din in the dining-room like a pain, the big tins of rice pudding sloshing down the tables. Penn had been sounding off about having to look at Smeeton, who was sitting opposite him, for the whole fifteen minutes of eating-time. 'It's enough to put anyone off their food. Those pimples!'

Smeeton, smarting, brought up the subject of Mitchell. Fletcher said to him, 'Tell us about what goes on in Oakhall, Smeeton, what your cousin says.'

Smeeton's cousin was at Oakhall for stealing cars. Conversation concerning the privations of life at Oakhall, as related by Smeeton, had a gruesome popular appeal, and everybody except Penn liked to hear the tales.

Penn said, 'We don't want to hear about Oakhall, Smeeton.'

'Oh, yes, we do,' said Fletcher.

'You get up at five-thirty,' Smeeton said, stirring mounds into his rice pudding, smiling, watching Penn, 'have a cold shower and do PE for an hour outside, in just shorts. Even in the rain. Old-fashioned sport, press-ups and knee-bends and crippling suchlikes. Go in and have another cold shower, get dressed, inspection just

165

like in the army. Baked beans for breakfast every day of the year. Get changed again. You spend all day getting changed and washing. Scrub floors all morning—'

'We don't want to hear about Oakhall, Smeeton,' Penn said.

'Stew for lunch, thin and greasy.'

'Like you, Smeeton.'

'Every day of the year, never any different. Drill after lunch, like in the army, round and round, up and down, ex-army sergeant major.'

Penn put his spoon down. 'Shut up, Smeeton.'

'Wash and change,' said Smeeton. 'Go and dig the kitchen garden.'

Penn said to Maxwell, next to him, 'Pass the rice pudding down.'

'Pass the rice pudding down,' Maxwell said.

'Bread and marge for tea.'

The rice pudding, very full, came sploshing up the table and stopped opposite Penn.

'After tea, lessons, six till eight. Wash again.'

Penn got up, kicking back his chair. He leaned over the table and put both hands round the back of Smeeton's neck, linked his cast-iron pianist's fingers, pulled Smeeton bodily out of his chair and pressed his face down into the rice pudding. The dish served twenty-four, and Smeeton went in over the ears. Penn went on holding him, while everyone watched, goggle-eyed.

'I say, Penn—' Maxwell began.

Bates was laughing. Smeeton's flailing arms knocked over a water jug and a plate of pudding into Fletcher's lap. Fletcher jumped up and jabbed his fork into Penn's hand and Penn let go and got Fletcher by the wrist, jerking up his arm so that Fletcher went over backwards. Smeeton lifted his head, choking out rice pudding in all directions, and Penn ducked him again, until Maxwell tapped him on the arm.

Soggy had arrived, and the dining-room was silent as a tomb, save for Smeeton drowning.

'Get out, Pennington,' Soggy said, his voice shaking. 'Go up to Mr Stack's room and wait for me there. Fletcher, get up. Take Smeeton out. Maxwell and Bates, get a cloth and clear up this mess.' His eyes flamed at Penn; Penn expected to see a forked tongue flick out. 'Never, in all my forty years of teaching, have I seen such an appalling display of irresponsibility. Get out of my sight, Pennington, *quickly*!'

Penn got out. It was worth it, whatever happened.

'He didn't!' exclaimed Peach, beaming at the thought. 'God, I wish I'd been on duty. What a lovely sight it must have been. What's Marsh going to do now?'

'God knows. What can you do with a boy like that?' Matthews was searching Soggy's desk with a worried frown between his eyes.

'Smeeton's half drowned,' he said. 'In rice pudding, of all things. What an accident to write up in the First Aid book! Look, Peach, has anyone had the First Aid brandy? I can't find it anywhere.'

'Not that I know of. It should be under the petty cash.'

'Well, it isn't. That's where I put it back, last time.'

'Who's swiped it, then?'

'It was a half-bottle, near enough full. Have I got to report a theft as well?'

'The only person I've seen under the influence around here lately is Bates,' Peach said.

'You mean we're back to Pennington again? It's just as likely to be someone on the staff. Three-quarters of us are boozers. I'd better make out it's used up. We don't want any embarrassment, do we? Miss Harrington, probably. She's got a nose like a port-hand light. Smeeton can make do on sal volatile.'

'I wouldn't waste brandy on him. It's Marsh who'll need it, if he's dealing with Pennington. I reckon that boy's got Marsh beat.'

'Marsh has no idea. Pennington's obviously not going to get his ruddy hair cut in time for my swimming gala, thanks to Marsh's interference. It's enough to make a man weep. Don't say anything about the brandy, Peach. There's enough trouble in this place without our turning up any more.'

In spite of the Education Committee's distaste for corporal punishment, Penn had some difficulty in making himself comfortable on the piano stool when he eventually turned up for his music lesson.

'Where've you been? We've plenty to get through. The nineteenth isn't far away now,' fussed Crocker.

'Mr Marsh kept me,' Penn said. 'It's not my fault.'

'That man's always interfering. What are you doing this afternoon? Are you free to play?'

'Yes. It's swimming.'

'Good. Don't you get your hair cut before the nineteenth, whatever happens, Pennington. Now, what were you doing this morning? The arpeggio exercises? You really do need to concentrate on this octave section more than anything else. It's the arm action that matters. I've told you all this. Shoulders taking the arm weight so that the whole arm is relaxed and light and you get a good free vibration right down, in and out of the keys on a good oblique angle. You can do that for half an hour when I leave you. Start fairly slowly with the metronome and step it up. I think the rest of it is coming along quite nicely, apart from the fact that you don't treat it with the delicacy it deserves. You do know what it's about, don't you, Pennington?'

'Well . . .'

'You've heard the scherzo from Mendelssohn's music to "Midsummer Night's Dream"? It must have the same fairy-like quality, Pennington. Fast and light and soft. Not bashing the ball out to Maxwell at right-half. Keep your physical beef for the closing passage.'

Penn sighed.

'I've sorted out some pieces here which I want you to begin on right away, all very light and delicate . . . this Chopin study, opus twenty-five . . . some more Mendelssohn, "The Bees' Wedding" and "The Spinning Song". Very good stuff for you. Chopin was the finest pianist of his time, yet he had no physical strength at all, Pennington. You could bear it in mind. I'm not suggesting you pretend you're dying of consumption, but you get what I'm driving at?'

'Yes, sir.'

'Less of the Polonaise in A major and the Revolutionary and a few more pieces in the nocturne style, I think. Even the Polonaise doesn't have to be played as fast and as loud as you play it.'

'I like it that way.'

'Mr Marsh doesn't, I'm afraid. Not in the hall, at

least. If you promise to work, Pennington, you can go back to playing in the practice room, and give them all a rest.'

'I don't mind playing in the hall,' Penn said, pleased that he was driving everybody mad.

'Very well. I must say it's a much better instrument down there. You're working very well, Pennington. Working. Several people have remarked upon it. I'm not the only one to have noticed.'

Faced with periods of two or three solid hours at the keyboard, Penn had found that working was less boring than not working. He had noticed himself that he was working, and been amazed. He pretended that he wasn't impressed by his progress, but he had to admit that he had surprised himself. He had so much time now to think about it. There were times when he even thought he was enjoying it, but this heresy he would stifle the instant it stirred.

'Look, this festival thing,' he said to Crocker. 'I don't want to go in the Open. I'm doing something else that day.'

'You're joking, of course,' Crocker said, looking like a nervous horse.

'No, I'm not.'

'Pennington, I'm not giving you the choice. You're going in for it.'

'There's something else I've got to do,' Penn said.

'You can do something else another time.'

'No, I can't. It's the same day.'

'You're not doing this to me, Pennington,' Crocker said. His voice shook slightly. 'You can do it to Stack and Marsh and even Matthews, but not to me. Not now.'

Penn didn't know what else to say. Strangely, he was on Crocker's side, in a way. But he was going to the Folk Festival just the same.

'You can't do exactly what you want all your life, Pennington.'

Penn was indignant. 'But I don't! I do what other people want all the time. That's what gets me—'

'And what would you do if you could do exactly what you wanted?'

This had floored Penn before now. He had no answer. He was angry and sullen. 'I wouldn't do this, for a start.'

'No, you ignorant child, and I wouldn't do this!' Mr Crocker's venom startled Penn. 'But we're stuck with it, Pennington. Both of us. And we must make the best of it. And let me tell you, Pennington, that this gift God gave you, which you are too thick-headed to acknowledge, is the one and only grace you possess, or are ever likely to possess, and while I'm stuck with my part in this ill-conceived system, I'm going to make quite sure that you're stuck with yours. So get on with it! You're wasting time, Pennington. You've only got *two hours* today, and there's a lifetime of work ahead of you——'

Penn thought, The old fool's bonkers, and lifted his hands and drowned Crocker's voice in the thunderous passage that closed the Mendelssohn piece. He felt as if he was sitting on a bed of nails. Cripes, he thought, roll on, old age! The next two hours, he felt, would see him there.

CHAPTER EIGHT

PENN FELT PRETTY desperate, taking stock of what was happening to him and unable to deflect the inexorable course of his fate by any means whatever.

Getting dressed the following Saturday evening to go to the folk club meeting at the barge, he was more conscious of Mitchell than of Sylvia, his mind returning all the time to the question of how long he had before he was charged with either the offence he hadn't committed or the offence he had. He could not believe that Mitchell was so stupid that he would not find out about the ride to school on the borrowed Honda. And when he did, that meant he would land up in Oakhall.

Penn stared gloomily into the mirror, combing his hair. It was true that he didn't know what he did want to do, but equally well he knew what he didn't want to do. Oakhall was top of the list there. If, by a great effort, he was able to move his thoughts from this priority, he found no cheer in the fact that, since his father had received the Jaguar bill, he had stopped paying his son any pocket money. Penn had exactly sixpence with which to woo Sylvia.

He went downstairs and took his mother's purse out of the sideboard drawer. It had four pounds in it. Penn took one, and put it in his back pocket. His mother came in and saw him.

'Just give me that back, you thieving—' She swore at him, her high Irish colour flaring up with rage.

'No, I won't,' Penn said. 'If you want it, you can take it off me – if you can.' He stood with his back to the sideboard, glowering at her, knowing that she could not touch him, hating her.

She shouted at him, bringing in Oakhall again. Penn felt the violence rising up in him.

'It's your fault I haven't any money, isn't it? Making me stay on at school! What am I supposed to do, go to bed every night when I come home? I haven't had a penny for over a month. I haven't been out anywhere for weeks, have I! I haven't even got anything for a coffee or fags or *anything*. I might as well be in Oakhall already as go on here!'

Self-pity flooded him, listening to himself. His righteous indignation must have touched his mother, for she paled down, merely breathing hard.

'I haven't even got a decent shirt fit to go out in,' Penn said, knowing his mother, pressing hard. 'And my bike needs a new tyre – I can't use it. I've got to hitch to Northend tonight. I might as well be dead, at this rate.'

'I'll give you some money for a haircut,' his mother said.

'Well, I've told you, haven't I? I can't get it cut now. They've made a thing about it at school, that old Soggy – you know him. If I back down now it's just being chicken. He'll gloat. They're on at you all the time, I've told you, just like being in the army or something. Why should I? It's a free country, isn't it?'

'What's it got to do with them?' his mother asked. 'You mean they've told you to get it cut?'

'Yes, I'm suspended games and everything. Can't be in the swimming gala—'

'That's a flaming liberty! Who do they think they are, then?' His mother was getting all red again.

'Well, I've told you. What with them, and Dad going on at me, and you – Oakhall'd be a rest cure.'

'Oh, Pat, don't say that. Your father'll get you out of it.'

Penn knew he had won.

'Here, take another pound. I'll talk to your father about the pocket money. And don't do anything about your hair. Not if that's the way it is.'

Penn took the money and went, without another

word. He called for Bates and they walked up to the main road and got a bus. Now that his hair was so long, hitchhiking wasn't easy any more. People looked at him and drove on. In fact, Penn found his hair a darned nuisance, what with washing it and swimming, but he knew he was stuck with it now until the end of term. He was silent and morose, and Bates let him alone. He was thinking about Sylvia, and all his nerve went. He didn't know anything about girls, or how you made them interested in you. He only knew that he just wanted to stare at her.

When they went down into the barge it was quite crowded. There were a lot of girls, as well as Sylvia, but Penn didn't notice them. Bates, not worried at all, went up to Sylvia and said, 'Look, we've come.' Penn said nothing.

'Oh, John, how nice,' Sylvia said, smiling at Bates. 'I told Colin about you. I'm glad you've come.'

Colin was the guitar player, dashingly handsome. Penn, watching Sylvia, could have strangled Bates for the 'John' and the smile. For himself there was an uncertain half-smile, no more. Plunged in gloom, he leaned against the wall, his hands in his pockets, listening and scowling. Bates brought him a beer. There was a lot of singing and strumming, and a new song practised, Sylvia sitting beside Colin and laughing with him. She

wore a very short silvery sort of dress, and her thighs
were slim and brown. Penn couldn't stop watching her.
He wished he were dead.

When the evening was well under way, and Penn
had got more and more miserable, Sylvia came over to
Bates and asked him to sing. Bates didn't seem to have
any more inhibitions – Penn supposed the school
concert had been good for his ego – and it was he who
stood up and said to Penn, 'Come on, what's the matter
with you?'

Penn took out his harmonica without a word. He
felt stunned. He played with such haunting despair that
'The Butcher Boy' was a sadder story than even he
remembered it. When they had finished there was a very
respectful response.

'I say, that was very good indeed,' Colin said,
obviously impressed. 'Are you coming to the Tolchester
festival? If you can repeat that, the Old Barge Club will
be able to put out a very good programme. Sylvia said
you were good, but that was really something.'

'Of course they're coming,' Sylvia said. 'I told you
the date, didn't I?'

'Yes, but—' said Bates.

'Yes, we're coming,' Penn said.

Sylvia looked at him for the first time. Her eyes
were green like the splintered, cloudy edge of a

broken beer bottle. She said, 'What's your name?'

'Penn,' said Bates.

'Patrick,' said Penn.

She pushed back a wing of silver hair. Penn wondered if it was real, that colour.

'Will you play for me?' she said. ' "Freight Train?" Or – no – "Will ye go, Lassie?" '

Penn nodded. He didn't know it, but wherever she went he would go, too. Colin started on the guitar and Penn waited for Sylvia, hitching his backside on a table, watching her shape under the silver dress. He had no breath for the harmonica. The melody communicated; he played with it and over it, embroidering the voice, watching the white curve of her cheek, feeling dislocated.

When it was finished, Colin said, 'You play that thing very well. You play anything else?'

'Only the piano.'

Sylvia smiled at him. Penn felt his face burning. What did you do, he wondered? What did you say? There was nothing inside him except a painful incoherence.

'Colin, perhaps he could play with us at the festival? It goes well. How about trying "O, Waly, Waly"?'

Penn watched her again, singing, finding the sad, nebulous tune with his tongue.

'There is a ship that sails the sea,
She's loaded deep as deep can be,
But not so deep as the love I'm in,
I know not if I sink or swim.'

Penn was sinking, and knew it.

Colin liked it, and said, 'Come down next Saturday and we'll work on it. It could be all right with the harmonica.'

Sylvia went away with Colin, giving Penn another half-smile. Another girl was singing, but Penn wasn't interested.

'Come on,' he said to Bates. 'Let's go home.'

'What's wrong with you tonight?' Bates asked.

'Nothing.'

'You didn't mean it about going to this folk thing on the nineteenth? Not with Mr Crocker and—'

'Yes, I did mean it. I've already told Crocker.'

'He didn't wear it, surely?' Bates was incredulous.

'Well, I told him, and he can't say I didn't warn him.'

'He'll go berserk if you don't go to the piano thing.'

'Well, that's his affair.' Penn was short, thinking of Colin touching Sylvia, taking her home, easy and good-looking, and Sylvia smiling, and her cloudy green eyes and her thin, silver body. Mitchell was out of his head, a moon-shot away.

'Oh, cripes,' said Bates, understanding. 'You, of all people! Fancy *you*—!' He went ahead down the gasworks jetty, kicking a lump of coke, choked with disgust.

Bates went into the music room where Penn was working with Crocker and waited, hopefully.

Penn was saying, 'This thing you gave me. The Chopin study, opus twenty-five, number two. I don't get it. It says two-two, but the left hand looks like six-four and the right hand looks like four-four to me. Why couldn't he write it in six-four and get rid of these silly triplets in the right hand?'

'You might not believe it, Pennington, but Chopin knew what he was doing. Difficult, granted. You have to feel the right-hand groups of triplets against the left-hand in six. Two large beats will help. You've got to feel two rhythms at once.'

'So it's really like two against three enlarged?'

'Mmm. Yes. Put your thumb here, like this, on the start of each of these groups of three. On each C. Try it. That's it.'

Bates coughed and said, 'Excuse me, sir.'

'What is it?' Crocker turned round testily.

'Mr Marsh wants Pennington, sir. He's got to come to the swimming gala.'

'But I'm not swimming,' Penn said.

'You've got to spectate. All the fifth forms are going to spectate and he said to fetch you. The bus is waiting.'

'Oh, God,' groaned Crocker. 'What we're up against! Get along, Pennington. Go and spectate. Don't work too hard at it.'

Penn got up. Strangely enough, he was annoyed at having to leave the piano just at that moment, having got into a frame of mind to carry on for the next two hours. The fact that he was reluctant amazed him. He followed Bates, wondering whether he was getting hooked by this habit of work. The idea worried him. Just brainwashing, he thought. The uneasiness stayed, to accompany all the other uneasinesses with which his mind was filled: Mitchell and Soggy and Sylvia and not going to the competition. Worrying was new to him and he did not like it. He stared out of the bus window and Smeeton said to him, 'What are you thinking about, Pennington? As if I couldn't guess. She's blonde and flat as a pancake.'

Penn swung round and hit Smeeton, crashing his weasel face against the window so that his jaw sagged.

'*Pennington!*'

Soggy stormed out of his seat, blue with apoplexy. He reached over Bates and dragged Penn to his feet by a handful of hair.

'Get out of your seat! Go and stand up at the front by the door. You're not fit to take out in public! You're untrained, Pennington, you're not even civilized! You are activated by the brain of a Neanderthal man. You are—'

Penn had heard it all before. He lurched down the bus and stood by the driver. The driver said, jerking his head towards the tirade, 'Something biting him?'

'He can't help it,' Pennington said tolerantly.

Very softly, but just loud enough for Soggy to hear, he whistled a few bars of 'Tannenbaum'.

At the baths Penn sat at the back of the crowded spectators' gallery with Maxwell and Crombie and Bates, and they started a game with the cards Maxwell had brought. With the six Northend schools participating, the baths were frantic with excitement, but Penn, ostracized from what would have been his day of glory, was determined not to take an interest. They could all drown, as far as he was concerned. Especially Soggy, who was sitting with Mr Stack and the other head and senior masters in a row along the bathside, near enough – Penn noticed with satisfaction – to get wet. Matthews was the starter. Penn did not look up from his cards as the first gun went.

By three-quarters of the way through the afternoon

Penn had won a florin and the Beehive was ahead by two points.

'Cripes, it's hot in here!' Maxwell complained. 'Your go, Bates.'

'Northend Parkside will go ahead if Turner doesn't win this.' Bates had to yell to pierce the girls' screaming.

Matthews was looking grim. Turner came third.

'You shouldn't have played that king, you ruddy fool,' Penn said to Bates. 'You knew Crombie had the ace.'

'There's only the four hundred metres freestyle after this, and Parker'll never get that. So if Burton doesn't get this one, we've lost the cup.'

'Hearts are trumps, Bates, you ruddy idiot! Cripes, I *need* the money, Bates, even if you don't. Bates, you are activated by the brain of a Neanderthal man.'

Penn groaned, loosening his tie. The humid, chlorine-laced atmosphere shivered to the tension of the Beehive spectators scenting imminent disaster. The girls' screaming reverberated round the acoustics like the sound of a panicking parrot-house.

'Pennington, Mr Matthews wants you downstairs.' A boy appeared at Penn's elbow, eager sweat shining. 'He says hurry.'

'You're joking,' Penn said sourly.

'No. Honest I'm not.'

'Crikey, Penn, go on!' Maxwell said, foreseeing a row of really resplendent proportions if the omens were correct.

'Hurry!' said the messenger, hopping on one foot. 'He said hurry!'

Penn went, not hurrying, but scowling hard, hands in pockets.

'He can only want him for one thing,' Maxwell said, eyes gleaming. 'What do you bet me? Can you see Matthews? Yes, there he is, worried as hell.'

'You mean the four hundred metres?' Bates said, aghast. 'He wouldn't!'

'If Burton wins this one, he won't. If Burton doesn't win, he will. Matthews is starting them now. You watch. As soon as they're off he'll go out of the swing doors to intercept Penn.'

He did. There was no sign of Penn, but Matthews's demeanour was enough to go by. He was bristling with anxiety, watching Burton's failure with glazed, suicidal eyes. Northend Parkside screamed and stamped until a baths attendant warned them about the condition of the gallery. In the front row, Mr Stack and Mr Marsh exchanged sporting, congratulatory smiles with the Northend Parksides. The loudspeaker crackled with the results, which gave Northend Parkside a lead of two points over the Beehive.

'Only a win in the last race will give us the cup,' Maxwell said, agog. 'Win or nothing. Poor old Penn! He's in for it! You watch. And old Matthews will be minced, utterly minced, by Stacker. Just watch Stacker's face when he sees Penn. And old Soggy's! God, this is lovely. Gorgeous!'

Bates was rather more dubious. 'You don't really think—?'

Maxwell did. There was still no sign of Penn, although the other five competitors for the last race were jogging about by the starting-blocks.

The loudspeaker began to intone: 'Senior four hundred metre freestyle. Competitors are as follows: Lane one, Northend Parkside, N. G. Peterson. Lane two, Market Road Comprehensive, P. R. Stubbs . . .'

'There he is,' Maxwell said, in a tone of the deepest satisfaction.

Penn had appeared out of the doorway to the changing rooms on the side where he was hidden from Stacker and Soggy. He was in swimming-trunks, biting the side of his thumbnail with some anxiety, watching Matthews, who was standing with his starting-gun at the ready. The other five competitors were already on their marks.

'Lane six, Beehive Secondary Modern, P. E. Pennington.'

As soon as the loudspeaker finished, Matthews raised his gun and bawled, 'On your marks!' Penn stepped forward, came to the block, and dived as the gun went off, all in one fell swoop. From the Beehive section of the gallery a shrill scream of glee went up, 'Pennington!' Maxwell clutched Bates in ecstasy.

'Look at Soggy! Look at Stacker! Oh, what bliss! What makings of superb, undiluted head–rolling!'

Bates looked, doubtfully. Soggy was white as a sheet, goggling at Penn as he passed by three feet away, shaking Penn's spray off him as if it were drops of blood. Stacker's face was expressionless, glazed, barricading his thoughts from the breathless gaze of the whole of his senior school in the gallery above. The delight of the gallery was ecstatic. Matthews, Bates noticed, had disappeared from sight.

'But it's not Penn's fault,' he said, looking ahead. 'He's only doing what he's told.'

'If he loses,' Maxwell said, 'he might as well drown.'

'Oh, he won't lose,' Bates said, his faith in Penn boundless.

'He's going to have a job. That's Peterson swimming for Parkside.'

Penn was swimming at a pace that suggested that his line of thought was very much in accord with Maxwell's. At the second turn he was his own length ahead of Peterson and various other lengths ahead of everyone else, swimming with little grace but extraordinary power, pushing up a bow wave that travelled up the side of the bath with him like the Severn bore. Soggy watched him pass and repass like a snake watching a rabbit. He said something to Stacker. Bates could guess at the hiss of his voice, the familiar venom. He felt a deep, sad sympathy for Penn.

So did Crombie. 'Poor old Penn. Four hundred metres, and he only came for a game of cards.'

Peterson came up until he was riding at Penn's shoulder, his stroke very easy. At the fifth turn they were almost a length ahead of all the others. Parkside started to shout, and the Beehive, who had been shouting right from the start, raised the pitch of their noise, which echoed with painful effect through the torrid dome of the Northend Municipal Baths. Stacker got out a handkerchief and patted delicately at the sweat of rage on his brow.

'Oh, cripes,' said Maxwell, as Peterson drew level. His glee had turned to the same agony as that afflicting the rest of the Beehive spectators. Only the Beehive spectators knew exactly why Penn had to be the winner.

Peterson, on the next turn, went ahead. Bates

wondered if Penn knew he was there, he surely could not see anything for hair. Bates felt almost like crying. He prayed for Penn to win, screwing his eyes up, but still looking. Penn, on the sixth turn, drew up with Peterson again, and they turned as one, twisting like otters. Peterson's stroke was now frantic, the elegance abandoned, but Penn's was no different, only more rapid. He put his head down and appeared to Bates to do the last length without another breath, drawing all the water in the bath after him, to leave all the others floundering through his triumphant wake. Peterson's head was at Penn's hips when Penn touched the bar. Bates found that he was crying, but they were all so sweaty nobody noticed.

Penn was so whacked when he finished that he stayed where he was, holding the bar, head down. He had this feeling, very strongly, that the only safe place was under the water, where it was blue and silent and unapproachable, and he did not want to come up, or climb out, or hear anything. He stayed there as long as possible, in spite of the tumult going on above him, but when everyone else had finished and climbed out, he was forced to make a move. He brought his legs under him and stood up. Soggy was standing right in front of him; Penn looked up and saw him from a new eye-level, and saw all the hairs in his nose bristling with anger, and the scraggy, drawn tendons of his neck standing out like handrails up from his tie.

'Pennington, I—'

Penn put down his head and flung back his hair with splendid effect, spraying Soggy from head to foot. Then, because the instinct was so strong, he pulled up his legs, twisted round and submerged again, and swam right down to the other end of the bath, under water. When he saw the steps at the deep end, he surfaced, climbed up them, and made his exit through the nearest doorway. He found himself in the women's changing rooms.

'Who do you think you are?' said the attendant indignantly.

But it was empty, the girls' events having finished earlier, and Penn refused to move, knowing that Soggy was unlikely to pursue him into so embarrassing a setting.

'I'll get the manager,' said the woman.

'You can't bring him in here,' Penn said, sitting down on the attendant's chair. He put his elbows on his knees and sat, hands dangling, feeling curiously divorced from his actual situation, as if he were not in trouble at all, as if he were still in the music room, working out the rhythmical subtleties of Chopin's Etude.

'Creatures like you,' said the attendant, eyeing the curling tendrils of hair which dripped over his shoulders, 'make us wonder which changing room we're in half the time.'

Penn could think of several good replies to this and even a demonstration, but as they were all obscene he contented himself by saying, 'Oh, get stuffed.'

'What school are you from?' she inquired frigidly.

'Northend Parkside,' Penn said.

She went away, and Penn looked out, saw that the bathside was emptying fast, and that Stacker and Soggy had gone, and went out, padding back to the men's changing rooms. Matthews met him at the doorway.

'We've got an appointment with Stacker when we get back to school,' he said. 'Both of us.'

'That doesn't surprise me,' Penn said.

'You swam a splendid race,' Matthews said. 'Beating Peterson is something to be proud of. I knew no one else could do it. Look, you won't get into trouble, so don't worry. Get changed and I'll wait for you. The bus has gone. I'll run you back in my car.'

Penn could see that Matthews was a worried man. He got changed and went out to the car park. Matthews didn't say anything, but gestured to Penn to get into the battered little Ford he drove. Penn got in and Matthews put the ignition key in, but did not turn it, sitting throughtfully, staring into space. Penn waited.

'Look, Pennington,' Matthews said eventually. 'I'm sorry about this, but I want to ask you to do me a favour.'

Penn could see it coming. He, too, stared into space.

'After all, we won the cup. He can't say much, can he, if we go back, and you've had your hair cut?'

Penn was silent.

'I like my job here,' Matthews said. 'I don't want to have to move or anything. I've got a nice house on a mortgage, and the wife's having a baby next month. I'm due for a rise in responsibility pay next year, the way things are. I'm terribly sorry to ask you this.'

Penn said, 'I'm fed up with my ruddy hair, but it's Mr Marsh. I'll have plaits before I get it cut for him.'

'Yes, I can see that. I understand, believe me. But would you, all the same?'

Penn did not say anything, fed up beyond measure. He recalled the grotesque appearance of Soggy from underneath, Soggy manhandling him in front of Sylvia, Soggy rating him in the bus.

'He came to shout me out at the end of the race, and I didn't listen. He'll think I got it cut because I'm scared. Well, I'm not scared. Not of anything they can do.'

'Look, I know that. Suppose I tell him? Would that be all right?'

'What, you go up to him and say I'm getting my hair cut because *you* asked me to? Because of your mortgage and your wife and all that? You'd tell him? Tell him, as far as he's concerned, I'd like to grow it long enough to wrap round his neck—'

'Yes, all right. I'll tell him.'

'Even the last bit?'

'If you insist.'

'Yes. All right.'

Matthews drew a happy sigh, and started the car. 'Where do you go? I'll wait for you.'

'The one on the front, next to the Odeon.'

Matthews drove down to the front and parked the car. He groped in his pocket and pulled out three florins and a few sixpences.

'There you are.'

Penn looked at the money and said, 'It's twelve and six the way I have it done.'

'God, Pennington, don't be all night.' Matthews gave him a ten shilling piece. 'I want to get this over.'

Crocker was laughing his head off.

Peach said to him, quietly, 'Be a bit more ruddy tactful, can't you? Marsh doesn't think it's a joke.'

'I do,' said Crocker.

They went into the staff room together, into the

stale five o'clock atmosphere of stewing tea and cigarette smoke.

'I hear we won the cup!' Crocker said breezily. 'Splendid news, Mr Marsh. You must be feeling really bucked! I must congratulate Matthews. Where is Matthews?'

Soggy looked at Crocker with loathing.

'It's the first time I've heard you take any interest in sports results, Crocker. I wonder you knew the event was taking place.'

'I only knew because you deprived me of my pupil for a good afternoon's work, merely for the sake of spectating, as Bates put it. I hope he spectated with credit.'

'Are you being funny?' Marsh said, very tight.

'You can't deprive me of my games, Marsh, and the Education Committee doesn't approve of teachers being caned.' Crocker's voice was sharp and amused.

'My God, Crocker—'

Soggy was interrupted by Miss Harrington coming in and saying, 'I would never have believed it! I've just seen Pennington and he's had his hair cut. He looks so elegant I didn't recognize him.'

Everyone in the staff room turned round and stared at her.

'Never!' said Peach.

Crocker's good humour stopped, like a tap being turned off, and his face fell into its more habitual lines of bitter resignation.

'No!' he said. 'Oh, no! Why has he done that? The foolish boy!'

Soggy turned round, smiling. 'I'll tell you why he's done it, Crocker. Because he knows when enough is enough. He knows how far he can go. He is frightened of the consequences of this afternoon's little escapade, and hopes to make things easier for himself. In other words, he has given in.'

Soggy's eyes glittered with triumph. He laughed, pleased with Crocker's dismay. Miss Harrington's news had erased his bad humour as completely as it had shattered Crocker's glee.

'I must speak to Stacker about this situation,' Crocker muttered, making for the door. 'I must see Matthews. I must have more of that boy's time, hair or no hair. There is so little time left, just as we are getting somewhere.'

Soggy shook his head. 'You're not deluding yourself, my dear Crocker, that you are getting anywhere with Pennington?'

'I may be deluding myself, but yes, I am getting somewhere with Pennington.'

He opened the door, having reverted to his normal

image: that of a frustrated, absent-minded gnome. As he opened it, Matthews came in, looking extremely cheerful, and Crocker stepped back again. Matthews looked around at the inquiring faces, avoided Soggy's glance and said, 'Well, that wasn't so bad. I'm still on the staff.'

'You've merely held Mr Stack's authority up to ridicule in front of the whole school and given the school's worst influence since the year dot a splendid opportunity of turning himself into the hero of the afternoon – not bad, at all,' said Soggy grimly. 'Congratulations.'

'Thank you,' said Matthews quietly. 'And while we're at it, for Pennington to beat Peterson, who has swum for England, wasn't bad either, and as he is completely guiltless, for a change, of any of the disobedience that occurred this afternoon, it wouldn't be out of place for you, his form master, to at least refrain from baiting him about it, if not to congratulate him.'

Matthews looked as astonished at his own speech as all the other people who heard it, including Soggy.

'I shall congratulate him,' Soggy said acidly. 'On his haircut.'

Matthews looked uneasy.

Soggy went on: 'His defiance is not, it seems, as absolute as it appeared, which is greater cause for congratulations to my mind than winning the four hundred metres. I shall heap congratulations on him,' Soggy promised with an edge to his voice.

'I have something to tell you, Marsh, about that haircut.' Matthews was worried, on Penn's behalf, but it was a promise. 'It wasn't his idea to get it cut, it was mine. I asked him to do it, to help smooth the situation over for me. And he agreed to it, on the condition that I told you why he was getting it cut. In other words, he insisted that you knew he wasn't getting it cut because he was frightened of you. He said—' Matthews paused, wondering whether he was doing the right thing. 'He said that, as far as you're concerned, he'd like to grow it long enough to wrap round your neck.'

There was a silence so profound that the clatter of the caretaker doing the floors two storeys down came quite clearly. Matthews looked at Soggy and sensed that, perhaps, it might have been wiser to pass off to Pennington a white lie as to what he had told Soggy. Soggy turned and went out of the door without another word, his face tight with fury, his lips twitching.

Matthews knew he had made a mistake. Pennington had helped him, but he hadn't helped Pennington.

Peach started packing his briefcase, cheerfully unconcerned. 'I do like a homely, friendly atmosphere in a staff room, like we have here,' he said. 'I've always said — that's what I like about the Beehive, the way the staff work together with a will, always a helping hand, a cheerful smile—'

'Oh, shut up,' said Matthews.

CHAPTER NINE

PENN WENT TO school the next day, and suffered so much sarcasm from Soggy concerning his manly appearance that on Friday he opted out and stayed at home. He went down to the river and lay on the sea-wall in the sun, thinking of Sylvia. He told himself that Soggy didn't bother him, but he just didn't want to take any more. He had been working too hard, what with beating Peterson and the hours he had put in at the keyboard. He felt on edge, as if things were closing in on him. They were, in fact, and he knew it. There was a day to go before he saw Sylvia, and then a week again to the festival at Tolchester, but he didn't know, if Mitchell was still probing around, whether he would still be in the clear by then. He had heard – and was pretty sure it was true – that a Northend youth had been pinched for the motorbike incident at Fiddler's Creek, but he very much doubted if, with Mitchell ill-disposed towards him and nosing around like a stubborn bloodhound, he was going to get away with riding the Honda.

On Saturday, in the barge, they played 'O, Waly, Waly'. Sylvia gave him her half-smiles, but said very little to him, beyond what the practice demanded. She was friendly and easy with Colin, and even with Bates, but towards him she was very quiet, almost shy. He thought it was because he was such an oaf, not knowing even how to speak to her, let alone make a pass at her.

Just before she went, she said, 'John told me something about you're supposed to be playing in a piano competition next Saturday. But you said you're coming to Tolchester?' It was a question, and Penn recognized it as one.

'Yes,' he said. 'I'm coming to Tolchester.'

'I'm glad,' she said.

What did it mean, Penn wondered? Glad to have a harmonica in the act?

'Why have you cut your hair?' she said. 'I liked it.'

He shrugged. The answer to that was too long. She touched his shoulder in passing, and he felt fires go through him, and despised his frailty so profoundly that he wished he had never set eyes on her. It was all so ruddy useless, like everything else. Getting you nowhere. He hated himself, everything about him. Particularly what he was going to do to old Crocker next Saturday. He was set on Tolchester now, because of this damned sex-urge, and he was too callous to do the right thing, yet not callous enough not to feel ashamed. He was slipping, he thought, to care, and yet he did care. Pathetic old Crocker, who had forced him like a hothouse cucumber, was going to get a cold reward.

Morose, preoccupied, he spent Sunday going over *Mathilda's* engine, getting it to go again. Bates bought a gallon of petrol, and they patrolled the river once or twice, and Penn tried not to think about things.

He went back to school and spent most of the week in the music room, having been handed over to Crocker almost entirely for the period before the competition. This pleased him well enough. There were hours of concentrated work when, at least, he didn't have time to think about anything else, and periods when he accompanied for choir practice or the fourth form singing, which killed time and kept him out of Soggy's way. It was the lull before the storm, he thought. Crocker brought him a Beethoven sonata which kept him occupied most of Wednesday, but on Thursday afternoon the peace was broken when the subject was broached by a direct question.

'This rubbish you were talking last week, about going somewhere else on Saturday – just put my mind at rest, Pennington. You're such a bastard you might well have been serious. Are you intending to present yourself at the Town Hall on Saturday and take part in this competition?'

'No, I'm not.'

Penn found it hard to say, and could not look at Crocker. There was long, hopeless silence. When he eventually looked at Crocker, Penn saw that the old man's eyes were full of tears. He felt so embarrassed he could not go on sitting there, but had to get up and go out to the bog. When he came back, Crocker had gone.

'The old fool. As if it matters,' Penn said out loud. And he played the Andante and Rondo Capriccioso, as if it were the competition, and started work on the sonata again. An hour later Crocker came back. He looked his usual self.

'I have news for you, Pennington,' he said.

Penn looked at him, suspicious.

'Look here.' Crocker, standing at the window, gestured for Penn to join him. Penn went and looked out, and saw the white police Mini parked in the staff car park. The shock came so unexpectedly that he felt himself quiver. His stomach turned over, and everything Smeeton had said rattled round his empty brainbox, each word sharp as a dried pea, and about as invigorating.

Crocker looked quite jaunty. 'The police constable

has just taken a statement from Mr Marsh to the effect that he saw you riding some motorbike on the day of the school concert, which apparently was not yours to ride. Mr Marsh said his evidence could be used against you 'with pleasure', and if he'd asked me, Pennington, I could well have used exactly the same phrase.'

Penn, choked, turned away. He could picture Soggy's satisfaction. He thought, in that moment, that if he had one more day left to him at Beehive Secondary Modern, he would get even with Soggy.

'He also questioned Bates, and seemed to get a good deal of satisfaction from the answers. More than poor Bates got in giving them. Bates is a very poor liar, although he tried. You shouldn't corrupt a good boy like Bates, Pennington.'

Penn went out of the room. He locked himself in the lavatory and stayed there until everyone had gone home, except the cleaners, then he emerged and went home himself. He thought he might just get the weekend before he was charged if he was lucky, if Mitchell had plenty of work on hand. There had been a fire in Moorham, at one of the boatyards, and that ought to keep him occupied for a day, at least.

Mitchell did not call. Penn went to school on Friday, and was caught by Soggy coming back from assembly.

'Lessons as usual for you today, Pennington. Crocker

says you can have a day off, so that you are fresh for his competition.'

So Crocker had not told anybody about the impending defection . . . Penn was not surprised. It wouldn't do his ego any good, after all the effort he had put in. Matthews, after PE, said to Penn, 'Good luck tomorrow, Pennington, on this music lark.' 'You're just bound to win,' Maxwell said cheerfully. 'Bash 'em like you did Peterson.' 'Oh, Penn, can we come and watch?' the girls said. Only Bates did not say anything, watching Penn unhappily. He had confessed, bitterly, and wept again, because Mitchell had got the truth out of him about the motorbike.

'They had me in the staff room, and there was him and Soggy and Matthews and Crocker came in, and then Stacker, and Soggy was a pig, almost worse than Mitchell. They got me all tied up, and I'm such a rotten liar, Penn, I can't do it like you. I'm sorry, I'm terribly sorry.'

'Oh, stuff it. It was Soggy, more than you.'

'Yes. He must have seen you. He could describe the bike and everything. And he told Mitchell that he was only too pleased you were getting your desserts at last and that you should have been passed for Borstal when you took your eleven plus, and then Matthews told him the remark was uncalled for, and they started having a row — this was when Mitchell had gone, and they had forgotten I was still there. It was quite funny really.'

'Hilarious,' said Penn.

'What are you going to do?'

'Before I get booked, I'm going to do for Soggy.'

Bates opened his eyes very wide.

Penn wanted to humiliate Soggy before the whole class, as Soggy had so often done to him. He wanted to burst his pomposity, make him weep. There was nothing bad enough really, but there was a limiting factor: it had to be something that would not interest the police, for Penn had no desire for his three months at Oakhall to be improved into two years at a Borstal. He went into a huddle with Rees and a staunch Soggy-hater called Patterson. Everyone knew what was in the wind, and the class was full of a curious tension that made Miss Harrington say in the staff room, 'Whatever's got into 5C today? They're in the strangest mood.'

'When Pennington's gone,' said Soggy, 'we might get somewhere with them.'

For his part, he was full of optimism at the way things were looking.

In the dinner-hour Penn screwed a large hook into the ceiling above the classroom door. Rees was hammering a hole into the rim round the bottom of an enormous galvanized bucket which he had taken out of the cleaners' cupboard.

'It's what they do in the *Beano*,' Bates said. 'It'll never work.'

'Oh, won't it?' Penn said grimly.

They had several run-throughs, and Penn marked a chalk cross on the floor just inside the door. And another one a foot or two farther in.

'You must stand there, Rees, to stop him coming any farther. He's got to be on this first chalk mark, or it'll miss him.'

'I've got some rope,' Patterson said. 'I asked Matthews and he gave me some.'

'Did you tell him what it was for?' Penn asked, grinning.

'I said it was for Soggy.'

'Penn, you're not really going to?' Rita Fairweather said. The girls were all pop-eyed and giggling. 'He'll kill you.'

'I don't care what he does,' Penn said recklessly.

'Maxwell and Crombie have made the mixture,' Bates came up to report. 'They've got it in the chemistry lab. Maxwell says he's just adding a smell to it. Herbs, he said, to give it a bouquet. He wants to know, before he hands it over, whether you're going to promise you're taking full responsibility, Penn. He wants it in writing.'

'Yes, if he wants it.'

'Oh, Penn, you're not—' Bates knew he was chicken, but the sight of the mixture had brought the gravity of the operation home to him. He had thought it had all been a joke at the start. But he could see now that Penn was in no mood for jokes.

'What's in it?' the girls wanted to know.

'Soot, liquid manure, oil, blood—'

'Shut up, Bates. It's a secret recipe,' Rees said. 'We don't want everyone to know it.'

Maxwell and Crombie brought it up and everyone stared at it in awe.

'I hope that ruddy hook's strong enough,' Penn said, eyeing the ceiling.

'I must come and see,' Maxwell said. 'This I cannot miss.'

'Soggy has got to walk from 3C to get back here when the last bell goes. It should just give us time to get it fixed. Put the bucket in the cupboard, Maxwell. Pennington, you're to watch for Soggy outside. It would be criminal to waste it on the wrong man. Rees and I will rig it, then I'll operate it, and Rees can stand on the second chalk cross. And everyone else can stand back and cheer.'

'Oh, cripes,' said Bates. He was already pale as a dead leaf.

Penn tested how much weight the hook was up to with a bucket of water. Then he rigged up the pulley system with some more hooks, and fixed the rope on to the bucket. By which time the bell went, and the girls went to Domestic Science, and the boys to Gardening, where they spent most of the lesson looking for the liquid manure which they all knew was in the bucket in their classroom.

Penn, Patterson and Rees got away early and sprinted back to the classroom. By the time the last bell went, the bucket was in place and Penn already had his hand on the pulley rope which ran from the hole in the rim up to another hook at a suitably sharp angle, and down to Penn. The girls came in, cautiously avoiding the chalk marks, and stood in silence. Some of them were pale, and the more chicken characters packed up and went downstairs, unable to face the impending situation. Bates sat in a desk in the farthest corner of the room, looking at the wall. He was trembling, and didn't want anyone to notice.

'All set?' Patterson poked his head in from the corridor.

'Yes.'

'I hope it works after all this,' Rees said, taking up his position.

There was utter silence in the classroom. Twenty-five

of them stood as if carved out of stone, watching the door. Penn picked up the rope.

Smeeton said, 'Cripes, Penn, this'll do for you.'

Rees put his head in. 'He's coming!'

It worked all right. Penn had not gone to so much trouble to muff it right at the end. He pulled the rope at exactly the moment Soggy stepped on the chalk mark, and the awful, stinking, filthy black mixture poured out of the bucket with the smooth precision of hot steel from the smelter, its exact target the top of Soggy's head, where the long grey hairs were manfully smoothed across the bald dome. It parted over his crown and ran in glutinous streams down his face and over his ears and down into the back of his collar, then in rivers over the shoulders of his suit, being absorbed, in big globs and splashes, on to his trousers, in a film over his hands and the whole of 3C's English compositions. Penn, giving the rope a final jerk, hoped the bucket would follow up, braining him, but his handiwork had been too good to provide this final satisfaction. He dropped the rope, and stood with his hands in his pockets, taking in the beautiful sight, his face quite grave, composed, and utterly calm.

There was a silence, profound as the dark inside of a tomb. Then one of the girls started to laugh. It was a hysterical laugh, but it was music in Penn's ears. Rees, standing his ground, caught Patterson's eye over Marsh's glistening shoulder, and hiccuped. He turned away. Patterson curled up, leaning against the door jamb, his shoulders heaving, and the bolder girls started to laugh with their usual spluttering and squeaking. Taking courage, even the timid spirits let out horrified giggles, and in a moment the whole room was in an uproar. Only Penn stood, faintly smiling, never taking his eyes off Soggy's plight.

To give him his due, Soggy remained commendably calm. He put his books on the floor, groped for a handkerchief and wiped his face so that he could see what was going on. When he could see, he saw Penn. When everyone saw him registering, his mind coping, the uproar died down to a silence as tense as the one that preceded it.

'Pennington?' he said, his voice silky.

'Sir?'

'You did this?'

'Yes, sir.'

Soggy turned his head to Smeeton and said, 'Fetch my cane.'

Smeeton fetched it, smiling.

'Come here, Pennington.'

Penn went. He didn't care, for the image of Soggy, dripping with filth, would stay in his mind as a comfort for ever, until the day he died. It was the nicest thing that had ever happened to him and nothing Soggy could do now could take it away.

'Hold out your hand.'

It hurt, but Penn wasn't bothered. Soggy was up to six when Rita Fairweather said, in a strangled voice, 'But, sir! Penn's playing in this competition tomorrow!'

Nobody, least of all Penn, had remembered the significance of tomorrow. Penn involuntarily took his hand away, and everybody gasped, fascinated by the implications. Soggy paused, blinking. Penn could see the various possibilities chasing themselves through his mind. As he himself was the only one who knew that he wasn't playing in the competition tomorrow, he was more curious than horrified, and relieved, physically, that Rita had stopped Soggy.

But Soggy's reaction was unexpected.

'Hold out your other hand,' he said.

Penn did so, and got another stinging six.

Soggy then said to Rita, very smoothly, 'Pennington is old enough to know that certain courses will incur certain consequences. He is no longer a very small boy, without logic, although one would often think so from the way he behaves.' He then turned to Penn, the malice shining in his eyes, and said, 'I am sorry if you find you are unable to play in the competition tomorrow,

Pennington. Very disappointing after all the work you have put in. But I think you will appreciate that I felt bound to equalize – I would not like the punishment to have been as lopsided as your thinking. I've no doubt that what has happened will be a great disappointment to Mr Crocker, for which you have yourself entirely to blame, not me.' He smiled, transparently delighted that the caning had had a punishment value far and away beyond the simple infliction of physical pain. 'Come and see me on Monday morning, Pennington, in Mr Stack's office, after assembly. Mere caning is not, of course, the end of this.'

He picked up 3C's dripping exercise books and turned away, gratified by the horror with which everyone was regarding the consequences of the afternoon's work. At the door he paused.

'Pennington must learn to think,' he said softly, 'mustn't he, Pennington?' And went out.

In that moment, Penn, his satisfaction blasted, blind hate seizing him, vowed he would win that ruddy competition if it was the last thing he ever did in his life.

Without a word to anyone he turned away, fetched his duffle bag from his desk, and made for home. He got some food and changed his clothes and said to his mother, 'If anyone wants me, I'm out. And I'm not coming back.' He went down to the river, rowed painfully out to *Mathilda* and lay on the bunk in her cuddy, vowing damnation on everyone he could think of, from Soggy to poor chicken Bates, and Major Harmsworth – drinking his gin on the next mooring, admiring the peace of the evening.

CHAPTER TEN

BATES CAME OUT late, hailing him from the bank. Penn ignored him for a bit and then, because of the urgency in Bates's voice, he rowed out and fetched him.

'Mitchell's been to your house. I saw him,' Bates said.

'We'll push off, then, I don't want to know till Sunday,' Penn said.

They went aboard, threw off the mooring, and motored down towards Moorham, anchoring in a lonely spot above the town in the mouth of a small creek.

'We'll have to catch the bus in Moorham to get to Tolchester,' Bates said. 'You think we'll do it without getting spotted?'

'I'm catching the bus for Northend. You can go to Tolchester on your own,' Penn said.

'What are you talking about? I can't keep up with you.'

'I've decided to play in this old festival after all.'

'Why? Because of Soggy?'

Bates understood. Penn did not answer.

Bates looked at Penn's hands doubtfully. 'What about——?'

'Oh, they're all right,' Penn said. 'It won't stop me.' He had had them in a bucket of water most of the evening, but he wasn't going to admit to Bates that Soggy had put him to this inconvenience.

'What about Sylvia?'

'Well, what's the use?' Penn said. He didn't want to think about it. He didn't want to think about anything. He rolled himself up in a blanket and went to sleep.

The morning was grey, drizzling, and in accordance with Penn's mood. He motored the smack down to Moorham and picked up a buoy amongst the fishing-boats, on the assumption that they would be less conspicuous there than anywhere else. All the smacks looked the same to a twit like Mitchell. Besides, they could not get ashore anywhere else, having left Jim's dinghy on the mooring at Fiddler's End, but where the smacks moored was close to the ferry crossing. Penn knew that George, the ferry-man, would pick them up if they gave him a shout.

'Look,' he said to Bates, 'let's go ashore and get some bacon. I'm blowed if I'm going to starve. We can't sit here looking at each other all morning.'

The river and quay were virtually deserted. George

picked them up on the half-hour when they waved, and they mooched up to the nearest shop, bought some eggs and bacon, and went back to the quay. They had to wait for George, and while they were waiting, an elderly woman came up and stood on the quay beside them, gazing distractedly down the river.

Penn took one look at her and scrambled up hastily, kicking Bates in the bottom. It was Mrs Crocker. Unfortunately, before he could beat a retreat, she looked at him, and recognition dawned.

'Oh, Pennington, fancy you being here! I wonder if you can help me, dear. Have you seen my husband anywhere?'

'Not down here,' Penn said shortly.

'I'm worried to death,' she said. 'He went out last night and he hasn't come back. Fishing, I mean. He's always having trouble with that outboard. And he was in a state last night – something at school, I think. He was very upset, and said if he didn't get out and find some peace and quiet he'd go raving. So I said, "Very well, dear," thinking he'd be back in a few hours. It was a lovely night early on, very calm and a big moon. I thought it would do him good. And I haven't seen him since. I must say, I'm rather worried now.'

Penn did not reply. What was he supposed to do, he would have said, if he had said anything. Hadn't she learned by now, after a hundred years of married life, that the old fool wasn't safe to be let out on his own?

'If you've got your boat down here—' She was eyeing the eggs and bacon, summing things up; she knew they had *Mathilda*, blast her – 'I suppose you couldn't just go down and see where he's got to? He doesn't generally go far. If you've nothing else to do?'

She was a bit pathetic, like old Crocker himself. And they hadn't anything else to do until twelve, save sit looking at each other in the cuddy, Penn reflected gloomily. He might even have a chance to tell Crocker that he'd changed his mind, which would cheer the old fool up tremendously.

'OK,' he said.

Mrs Crocker's face lit up. 'Oh, thank you, dear. That's very kind of you. I should be so relieved.'

Penn, not used to having anyone thank him for anything, felt uncomfortable. He yelled at George, and George collected them. As the water widened between him and Mrs Crocker, he felt a lot better. He told George what they were going to do.

'That old madman?' George said. 'He should have drowned ten years ago, that cranky boat he goes around in.'

'I expect his outboard's packed in.'

'I wouldn't be surprised. He runs it on marmalade, judging from the state it's in.'

They went aboard. Penn got the engine going and chucked off the mooring, and Bates started to cook breakfast on the primus. It was ten past nine. The Tolchester festival started at three, and the Northend competition at five; they had plenty of time. Penn decided he would as well be standing at the helm of *Mathilda* reverberating down the river as anything else he could think of just at that moment; perhaps the old hag had done them a good turn. He held the tiller with his thigh, and studied the palms of his hands, flexing his fingers in and out. There was no doubt that Soggy's treatment was hardly going to help when it came to the widest stretches prescribed by Felix Mendelssohn, but it would be painful more than impossible. His fingers hadn't been touched, and none of the skin was broken, although the weals showed. Penn had hardly expected to get away with less, but he was damned if Soggy was going to have the last word on the matter. He'd just show him, the old beggar. After that, Penn did not know anything. Lately, along with the habit of work, he had taken to thinking ahead, and it had given him nothing but worry and foreboding. He must get out of these bad habits, before they did for him.

'I say,' said Bates, putting his head out of the hatch,

'there's an awful lot of water sloshing about in this old boat.'

Penn shrugged. 'You got breakfast yet?'

Bates disappeared, and came up a few minutes later with a plate full of bacon, some rashers burnt and some nearly raw, and two mangled, frizzled eggs.

'You seen him yet?'

'There's a dinghy out by the Pitt Shoal. Could be him.'

The Pitt Shoal was two miles off the mouth of the river, farther than Penn really wanted to go. They could hardly turn back now, but he wasn't sure how much petrol they had left in the tank. He shovelled in his bacon and eggs. There wasn't another boat in sight anywhere; the morning was grey and drizzly and the sea heaved unpleasantly. Penn wished they hadn't come.

Bates said, 'It looks like his boat. There's an anchor out. But where is *he*?'

Penn frowned. As *Mathilda*, swilling out on the last of the ebb, rattled towards the Pitt Shoal, he could make out the dinghy quite clearly. But it appeared to be empty. There was a hump of what looked like old oilskins, nothing else.

'Looks like that could be him, in the bottom of the boat. Perhaps he can't get the outboard to go, and is having a nap till someone turns up.'

'But he always carries oars. He's not that stupid.'

'Waiting for the tide to turn, then.'

When *Mathilda* was about fifty yards off, Penn gave a shout, and another, but nothing stirred.

'She's in pretty shallow water,' Penn said, seeing the danger. He put the tiller over, but had left it too late. *Mathilda*, rising up on one of the uneasy swells, dropped with a crack and stopped abruptly. Penn put the engine in reverse, but to no avail. Thick sand churned out astern, swilling away on the tide, but the old smack merely shuddered. She was on hard, having been travelling at quite a lick. Penn swore horribly. He put the engine into neutral, but it cut out. The sudden silence was unexpected, and ominous.

'Cripes, don't say we're out of petrol!' He scrambled below for the dipstick and tested the tank. The stick came up dry. 'Oh, cripes, we're in a fine mess now!' He was furiously angry, at Crocker, himself, and everything else he could think of. *Mathilda* heaved and thumped, her old timbers groaning.

'What about him, then?' Bates said, gesturing across to the silent, rolling dinghy. 'What do we do? Is that him, that heap?'

'How should I know? I suppose it must be. He must have died or something. If he was asleep, he must have heard us.'

'Died?' said Bates incredulously.

'Well, he takes pills when he gets all het up. Haven't you seen him? He goes all blue and white in turns. When he's cross.' Penn had good reason to know, having so often been the cause of the phenomenon. 'And Mrs Crocker said he was upset.' No doubt himself again.

'Well, what are you going to *do*?' Bates said, his face all screwed up and tremulous.

'Me do? Cripes, why me?' Penn was indignant.

'You came out to rescue him, didn't you?'

'Well, I like that!'

Penn could see it coming, what he had to do, and the indignation welled up at the injustice of it, of doing someone a good turn and getting all tied up, of running out of petrol, of putting the old boat aground. He started to take his clothes off. He was for ever taking involuntary swimming lessons, almost every day, for some reason or other. Never because he *wanted* to. His mind raged. Bates watched him, silent and pale. Penn took off his watch, which only went sometimes anyway, thanks to its earlier ill-treatment, and gave it yet again to Bates. The wind was cold and he felt the goose-pimples rising. He did not want to go out to old Crocker very much now that he thought he was dead, and he stood naked, shifting from one foot to the other, glowering at the water.

'Go on,' Bates said.

'Why don't you go, then?' Penn snapped. 'The water's not deep. I'm not hogging it if you want to go.'

He launched himself gingerly, miserably, off the stern. Ten feet off the smack the water was deep, which made him even more angry, because it meant that *Mathilda* had gone on a miserable cheating little spit, not the bank proper at all. Crocker's dinghy was anchored in deep water. Penn swam up to it slowly, and hooked his hands over the transom.

The old man was huddled in the bottom of the boat, either dead or unconscious. Penn could not tell. His face, what Penn could see of it, was a terrible colour. Penn's indignation turned into a rather sick, creepy feeling of panic. He had never seen a dead person before, let alone had to do something about it. A ridiculous fragment of knowledge came to him: that you put pennies on dead men's eyes to keep them shut, and he looked at old Crocker's eyes, and saw the lids flicker. They opened. Penn felt the hair rising up on the back of his neck as the familiar gaze regarded him from the bottom of the boat.

'Help me, Pennington,' the blue lips mumbled, and the eyes shut again.

'*Cripes!*' Penn felt as if a ghost had just confronted him. He was trembling all over.

He handed his way round the gunwale until he came to the bows of the dinghy and heaved at the anchor warp, but without anything but the water to brace himself on, nothing happened. He had to follow the warp out and swim down, break out the anchor under water and swim back with it. 'Why me?' his mind kept exploding. He was as cold as a dead fish. He humped the anchor over into the bows of the dinghy, and then swam back to the smack, pushing the dinghy in front of him, which was hard work. The dinghy was much too cranky for him to attempt to get in. All the way his mind was raging at this thing he had got stuck with, and the scary, panicky feeling was very close underneath. Bates, staring down from the stern of the smack, looked as stricken as he felt.

'Oh, cripes, Penn,' he said uselessly.

'Take the warp, for heaven's sake, and make the dinghy fast.' Penn's teeth were chattering almost too much for him to talk. When Bates had got the dinghy, he swam to the bobstay and climbed on board, with considerable difficulty. The cold wind blasted his bare flesh. He could have wept.

'Is he dead?' Bates asked.

'No. He said something.'

'What are you going to do?'

'Get dressed,' Penn said.

He dried himself on a blanket and put his clothes on again, still shivering. *Mathilda* was thumping and crashing, driving up on to the sand, the water sloshing about in her bilges. Every time she thumped, dollops of uneasy water splattered Crocker's recumbent form.

'We must go back to Moorham,' Penn said, biting his thumbnail. 'We'll have to see if we can get the outboard working. The trouble is, if I get in, I'll sink the blasted thing.' Penn had scaled fourteen stone eight pounds at the last weigh-in and was very conscious of the fact. Bates, at a bare eight stone, didn't know how outboards worked. Penn lay down on *Mathilda*'s deck and leaned precariously over into the dinghy. The two craft rolled together, going up and down independently on the swell, grinding together, and after about ten minutes of vain fiddling and tugging at the starting-rope, Penn, head down and full of petrol fumes, had to retreat in order to bring up Bates's queasy breakfast. Bates watched him in despair.

'Penn, what are you going to do?'

Penn groaned.

'Oh, Penn!' Bates cried out.

Penn got up and leaned against the shrouds, wishing he were happily unconscious like old Crocker. Crocker's outboard was about as much use as Bates's cooking.

'You'll have to row him home,' he said shortly to Bates. 'There's nothing else we can do.'

Bates looked incredulous. 'Me?'

'Yes, you.'

'Why me?'

'Because, one: if I get in that dinghy it'll have a freeboard of about two inches, whereas if you get in it'll have about four, which is two more inches farther away from getting swamped. Two: what will you do if you're left on board here? I can't see you getting the engine started again.'

'Well, I don't see you getting it started either without any petrol.'

'Someone's bound to come by before long and I shall shout and get some petrol, or get a tow. Buck up, Bates. It's no good saying you can't row, because you can row as well as I can, and the tide is on the turn. You'll have it under you. Even if you just sit there, you'll arrive eventually.'

'Oh, cripes, Penn, I can't sit there rowing a corpse.'

'He's not a corpse, idiot! Else it wouldn't matter, would it? But he will be if you dither about much longer. He ought to be in hospital. Get a move on!'

Penn drove Bates down into the dinghy, swearing at him bitterly. Bates groped round for the rowlocks, and Penn leaned over, holding the dinghy by the gunwale.

Old Crocker looked terribly uncomfortable, his head lolling about against the ribs of the boat, but it was impossible to shift him without risking a capsize, so Penn shoved the dinghy off bodily as soon as Bates got out the oars. Bates was white and gibbering. Penn watched him go, hunching himself down on the hatch, his elbows on his knees. What a flaming mess the whole thing was! His watch showed him that it was getting on for half-past eleven. Penn knew that the day was doomed.

After a few minutes he decided he should have put the anchor out about an hour ago. *Mathilda* was just driving up on to the sand, although the tide was now flooding. He dropped it over the bows, but knew that she would go on crashing and banging and driving up the sand for some time before her scope stopped her. By then she could well have fallen apart. Exploring below, he found that the water was over the floorboards and still rising. The probability that he was going to go down with his ship did not strike him as strange at all, only a perfectly appropriate way to end this disastrous day. He went below and made himself a cup of tea to try to get warm and by the time he had finished, the water was up to his knees. He was unmoved. He didn't care if he drowned.

Bates was a speck in the distance when he went up

on deck again, but there was no sight of anyone else on the face of the earth. He looked at his watch again. Twelve o'clock. The sea was smooth and dreary, the sky a uniform grey. He went on sitting there, wondering what was the use of being alive anyway. The Rondo Capriccioso could have been conceived on Mars, for all the relevance it had to him in his present situation.

It was half-past twelve before he saw a boat. It was a yacht coming in from the sea, beating very slowly into the light head-wind. With luck, it would come fairly close to him on its port tack. Penn watched it gloomily. It was a yawl. When it got nearer, he recognized it as Major Harmsworth's *Escape*. His faint optimism, which had stirred in spite of everything, keeled over and sank without trace. The trouble was, he thought, *Mathilda* would soon follow suit.

He got to his feet and waved a white teatowel on the foredeck as the yawl crabbed slowly towards the sand, carried on the tide. He doubted if the signal would be misunderstood, especially as *Mathilda* was now so low on her marks, but he was relieved when the yacht went about and hove-to. Major Harmsworth was looking at him through binoculars. Penn thought, Even after the Jaguar, he can't leave me to sink, the rat.

The fruity voice came over the water through a loudhailer, making Penn wince: 'We can't come in any closer and we have no dinghy. Can you swim?'

Could he swim! God in heaven, he spent half his life swimming! The old idiot had good reason to know he could swim anyway. Penn wasted no time, but dived off *Mathilda*'s stern and struck out for the yacht, watch and all. He wouldn't need his watch in Oakhall, according to Smeeton. When he reached the boat, he got the reception he had anticipated, cold as the grey water. He said nothing, letting Harmsworth's hostility slide over him. There was no point in explaining anything: he felt too cold to argue.

'I suppose you'd better go below and get dry,' the Major said at last. 'He can have that Aran jersey of mine, Humphrey, the one I use for painting in. And there are some slacks in the forward locker.'

Below, Humphrey was slightly more affable than the Major himself, producing a towel and the clothes, and lighting the Calor gas to make a cup of tea. He asked Penn what he was doing, alone on the sinking smack, but Penn, after the ratting he had got, was not disposed to make polite conversation.

'I was just out for a look round,' he said.

He glanced at the clock on the bulkhead. It was one o'clock. There was a bus to Northend at four, and one at six, but the wind had dropped light, and the yawl was making very slow progress. Penn expected the

Major to put the engine on, but the Major appeared to be in no hurry. Humphrey started to make a salad, and the Major spent a lot of time watching some stupid sea birds through the binoculars. Penn went up on the foredeck out of the way and lay down and went to sleep. He just didn't want to think about it any more. Old Bates would have been back long ago.

The Major anchored when he got back into the river and sat with Humphrey in the cockpit admiring the beauties of nature. They were too far out to make it worth Penn's while to go ashore, and he was tired of swimming. He lay listening to the murmur of the cultured voices, knowing that everything was finished for him, that he would not even have the satisfaction of levelling scores with Soggy. Not that he cared in any other way about missing the competition, for he hated playing in competitions; he hated the sacred atmosphere and the intense women with their hair in buns and the smooth boys with their nice voices – infant Major Harmsworths – who had smooth, nice relationships, with their music teachers ('Well *done*, Nigel!') and smiling, elegant mothers. He hated the way they gave him looks, because he wasn't their sort. But he had wanted to go, desperately. Lying there, his hands clasped behind his head, he thought it rather old that old Dotty was himself the reason for stopping his playing, the way things had turned out. He could not help feeling a bit sorry for the silly old beggar.

But, having plenty of time to think, he was sorrier for himself.

'You, up there! You might as well work your passage! Get up the anchor chain, will you? Young lad like you, plenty of beef—'

By the time he had got in the yawl's nine fathoms, he was very conscious of his hands again, stiffening and sore. But it didn't matter any more. It was half-past five. The competition had started half an hour ago. The yawl butted her way up the river under engine, the tide having turned against her. His own watch having stopped, Penn went aft and peered at Humphrey's. As they came up to Moorham it was ten to six. Penn began to bite the side of his thumbnail.

'If you wouldn't mind—' he said, hesitantly. 'If you could go close to the fish-quay, I'll jump for it.'

'I thought you lived at Fiddler's End?'

'I'm supposed to be playing in a competition at Northend. I might just catch the six o'clock bus.'

'And what about my clothes?'

'I'll bring them back to Mr Purvis's yard tomorrow.'

'Hmm.' But the Major put the tiller over, making for the fish-quay. His military eyes raked Penn, who stood on the side-deck, hands in pockets, scowling with the effort of being polite.

'Pity there's no military service any longer for young chaps like you. Do you the world of good,' the Major said. 'You get everything too easy these days, that's your trouble.'

Getting shot would have done the Major a world of good, Penn thought.

The yawl went into the quay, travelling fairly fast, and Penn jumped from the shrouds, catching the top of the wooden jetty with his hands and hauling himself up painfully. Once on his feet, he ran. The bus was at the clock tower, the driver just starting the engine. Penn leapt on and ran up the stairs. God only knew how many entries there were for the competition, but the Andante and Rondo Capriccioso took six minutes to play, and he would get to the Town Hall approximately one hour and forty minutes after the start of the competition. Allowing for the interminable time the judge took to make the hieroglyphics in his little book after each performance, he would, with luck, still be operating by the time the bus arrived. Penn put his feet up on the seat and tried to pretend that he had everything under control, but he was hollow with doubt. He was also hollow with plain hunger.

The conductor came up for the fares and Penn

discovered that the Major's trousers harboured no forgotten coins.

'Look, you know I've got a school pass,' Penn said urgently. 'For God's sake don't chuck me off.'

'Cripes, mate, I'm not a philanthropic society.'

Penn argued, spurred by the single-minded determination that had seized him since the Soggy incident. The bus conductor, who knew him well, got bored and said, 'Oh, well, stay on. I can't be bothered . . .' There were only two other people on the bus, both downstairs.

Penn sat with his arms clasped across his chest, hands in his armpits to keep them warm. He concentrated on the music, seeing it in his mind as it was printed on the page, humming the opening theme to himself. He took his hands out and stretched them and did silent scales all up and down the back of the seat in front of him. By the time the bus lurched into the Northend Broadway, Penn wanted to slam the Andante and Rondo Capriccioso more than anything else in the world; he had spent so many sweating hours on its cunning ways, wishing Felix Fiendish Mendelssohn frying in hellfire, writhing to his own tempo on the metronome, that the wretched piece had to be exorcized, offered up as sacrifice on the sacred Steinway belonging to the Northend Municipal Council, or else Penn felt that it would haunt him for the rest of his days. After the Mendelssohn and the thumbed pile of Bach, Mozart, Beethoven and Co. that spilled out of Crocker's cupboard entirely for his consumption, Penn thought Oakhall would be a haven of rest, in spite of anything Smeeton said. He got up and dropped heavily down the stairs as the bell rang for the Town Hall.

It was only as he went up the imposing staircase and came to the arrow pointing down the corridor to 'Open Pianoforte Competitors' that Penn became conscious of the fact that he was not exactly, in appearance, the most prepossessing of performers. The official standing outside the door of the Council Chamber, where the competition was taking place, eyed him coldly.

'What do you want?'

'I'm a competitor for the Open Pianoforte. Is it still on?'

'You can't come in here like that!' said the official, outraged. 'It started at five. The last competitor has just finished. Mr Smythe-Potter is working out the results now.'

'But I'm entered!' Penn said. 'I couldn't help being late! There was an accident – my music teacher's had to go to hospital – oh, look, *please*—' He put his hand on the door-knob, desperate. 'I'm sorry about my clothes, I couldn't help it! Please would you ask him?'

The official hesitated.

'It's very unorthodox. Who are you? Your name—?'

'Pennington. Patrick Pennington.'

'I'll go and see. Just step inside then, and stay by the door.'

They went inside together, into the hushed, nervous arena of hard chairs occupied by hushed, nervous pianists and their friends and relations. Penn smelt the tension, and saw the God Almighty judge sitting at his little table with a glass of water and sheets of notes, and the officials hovering, and the bored reporter of the *Northend Standard* doodling in his notebook with a Biro. The municipal Steinway crouched on the raised dais, malevolently impartial. Penn leaned against the door, stretching his palms against the pains that afflicted them, willing the God Almighty to give him his chance. The official conferred, and the God Almighty's gaze reached out to Penn as he leaned against the door, and considered him, while the official went on explaining. Penn, embarrassed by Major Harmsworth's paint-bespattered trousers and the highly unsuitable Aran jersey with the unravelled cuffs, straightened up and tried to look godfearing and acceptable. Everyone else in the room was staring at him.

The official beckoned. Penn padded down to Jehovah's seat, hearing the faint squelching of his wet plimsolls. Jehovah looked him up and down, cold and unwelcoming.

'Sit here,' he said, gesturing him to a chair. 'I'll hear you in a few minutes.'

Penn sat, resting his elbows on his knees, rubbing his hair back from his face. He felt drained and bleak and horribly alone. He would have given his most precious possession, his useless wet watch, to have had soppy old Bates sitting beside him in the abattoir. The watch stood at twelve fifty-two. Penn unfastened it and put in the back pocket of Major Harmsworth's slacks. Old Crocker could well be dead now, for all he knew. Penn wished it had been Soggy. He would have swum out to the dinghy and turned it over and held the cold blue face under . . . His hands *hurt* . . . Oh, cripes, what was the use? He fixed his mind on the opening bars of the Mendelssohn piece, feeling that this time, now, and tomorrow with Mitchell, he was really going down, foundering without trace. And there was nobody there even to see him go, let alone care.

'All right,' said Mr Smythe-Potter, nodding to him. He put his pen down and sat back in his padded, alderman's chair, and put the tips of his fingers together, and watched Penn walk to the piano. Everyone else in the audience watched, disapproving, and praying for calamity. Penn could sense the hostility. It made him feel almost at home. OK, Soggy, he thought, lifting his hands, hitching himself into position on the piano stool. I'll show you, you murky sadistic swine . . . He paused, scouring his mind clean of everything but the music, praying that out of his confusion and bitterness he could express the serenity of the Andante as if he had been lying on the sofa thinking of nothing but Mendelssohn's flaming fairies all afternoon. His hands started to play, very softly, smelling of Major Harmsworth's anchor chain, but responsive and obedient. Penn, enchanted by the Council's superior instrument, was immediately cut free from his anxieties, eager only to release the melody with the first stroke of his right fourth finger on the G sharp and let it fall as sweetly as he knew how into its shapely poignant pattern on the keyboard. This was the hardest part of the whole piece for him, for he was happier when the fireworks came and the old fingers really had to move, when the subtleties of dynamic control and *tempo rubato* which old Crocker had had him slaving over for the last two months stood down before the demands of sheer fingerwork. ('Ruddy technician!' Crocker would growl at him, piling on the Chopin nocturnes and preludes. 'Think boy, feel!' and Penn would curse with as much indelicacy as the music demanded delicacy.) Somewhere in his mind Penn had all this stowed away, and he knew now that mere technicians did not win competitions, and he played to warm poor Crocker's soul and to damn Soggy and to lift the Mendelssohn melody out of the County Council piano into the cold dome of the Council Chamber to stab the alien heart of Mr Smythe-Potter with its vigour and beauty.

Mr Smythe-Potter, watching Penn closely, opened his eyes very wide and tapped his forefingers slowly together to convey his emotion.

Six minutes of pure sweat, Penn thought, recapitulating on the Scherzo theme, and what to show for it but words in the Smythe-Potter notebook and the echoes fading out over the surface of the Victorian painting of 'Integrity and Labour' on the ceiling? Nothing in the hand, nothing ruddy anywhere, to show whether he had done well or failed, or even existed, yet never had he worked and felt and *thought* so hard. He came down the octaves with his tongue sharp between his teeth, his palms splitting, one or two inaccuracies proving that he was putting soul before mere perfection – or so he hoped. The mistakes stung him, but the sum total was rich and beautifully controlled. He knew he had nothing to reproach himself with at all.

As the last note faded, Penn heard his empty stomach roll forlornly, and realized that he was ravenously hungry. He also, with a fierce pleasure, knew that he had never played the Andante and Rondo Capriccioso any better. He got up and went back to his seat, and Mr Smythe-Potter went on writing on his sheets of paper in a very neat, small hand, lines and lines and lines. Penn, recalling past occasions, and the long, deadly rambling on each competitor that had to precede the actual results, slumped back in his chair and prepared to go into a coma for the next hour. Not having heard any of his rivals, he kept a weather ear open for undue praise on Smythe-Potter's part, but for the most part let the flat, dry voice ride over him. He was extraordinarily tired. Whether he won or not was out of his hands; strangely, knowing that he had played as well as he was capable of, it did not worry him. Even Soggy had shrunk, like the desiccated, tiny-minded carcass that he was, to infinitesimal significance. Instead, Penn felt a tender concern for potty old Crocker that surprised him. I could go and see him in hospital, he thought. And tell him I played. It might cheer him up. If he was still alive to be cheered up. Penn, sitting and not listening, but feeling strangely contented, wondered why he was no longer worried about things: even Oakhall did not seem very important any more. He supposed he was too tired to care.

'And so to the last competitor, P. E. Pennington . . . a pupil of the Beehive Secondary Modern and the youngest person to perform today . . .'

Penn sat up, and felt a cold goose-shiver creep up between his flesh and Major Harmsworth's jersey. If he slates me, he thought, I'll get up and mash him, the toad-voiced old beggar. He was thin and dry, in Soggy's blood-group . . . 'An extraordinarily accomplished performance, taken at a very ambitious tempo yet without loss of clarity . . .'

After the first shock, Penn found that the words were not registering. Praise came to him so rarely that he was incapable of understanding it for what it was. The old boy's playing me along, he thought; he's going to bring in the crunch at the end. But at the end Mr Smythe-Potter said, 'I am therefore placing this competitor first . . .'

Penn looked at him, his face tight with suspicion. He felt hollow and breathless, like being winded in soccer, when mere air was so desirable, and yet apparently unattainable. Then the professorial face smiled at him, and Penn realized that this was no sarcastic liar, like Soggy, having him on, but a normal human being congratulating him on his talent. He smiled back. He felt wonderful suddenly, in a way quite new for him. I must go and see old Crocker, he thought instantly. As long as Crocker knew, he didn't care a fig for Soggy.

He got up, after the other winners had been announced, and started for the door, but there were people in his way: an official telling him about the Mayoress awarding the prizes on Wednesday evening and he would be expected to attend, and the reporter wanting to know the story of his life, and an awful fluting woman asking if he was interested in joining her chamber group for Schubert evenings ('So refreshing, dear, if you've never played with other instruments . . . here's my address . . .'), and various fellow competitors saying congratulatory things which amazed him (quite the last thing he would have thought of saying to anyone who might have beaten him) . . . by the time he got to the door, the place was nearly empty.

Except for—

'Oh, cripes!' Penn said softly. 'What are you doing here?'

'I just wanted to see you,' Sylvia said.

CHAPTER ELEVEN

'WHAT FOR?' SAID Penn, almost as if it were a Soggy-trap.

'What do you mean, what for?' she said. 'What do you think what for?'

It was unanswerable. She was looking at him with those consummately improved eyes, smiling and tender, like in the figments of his wildest imagination. She put out her hand, and rested it on his arm.

'You said you *only* played the piano,' she said, slightly accusing.

'Why, did you hear it? Did you come on purpose? Bates told you?'

The hand on his arm had given him courage. They walked slowly down the mosaic-floored corridor under the portraits of the past fifty-odd Mayors of Northend Corporation, and Sylvia's hand moved down and took his own. Penn felt it, cold and incredible, against the dull throbbing of Soggy's canning. He remembered that he hadn't any money.

'Yes. He said you were going to play in this competition. He was late for the Festival. I thought neither of you was coming. He had some crazy story about some old corpse he'd had to row up the river – I thought he was raving. He is a weird boy, isn't he? Then he said you'd changed your mind, and weren't coming, and one of the boys had to come back early, so I asked him for a lift and I come here to see you instead. I sang first, so nobody cared.'

'Did Bates sing?' Penn, not daring to face the implications in Sylvia's speech, in case he'd got them wrong, asked a practical question.

'Yes, he did. Colin played for him. He's wonderful, isn't he?'

'Yes.' If Bates had got to the point of singing in public without himself to goad him, Penn was willing to concede this fact.

'But cracked,' she said.

'Yes.'

'But you,' she said, 'wasting time on the harmonica when you can do that. Any fool can play the harmonica.'

Cripes, she sounded just like Crocker! Penn looked at her warily. She smiled at him, no half-smile, but a sweet and tender whole smile.

'I think you're wonderful,' she said.

Cripes! Penn was afloat, drifting over the mosaic.

'I saw you at the swimming gala,' she said, 'and I cheered and cheered for you, and they were all cheering for Peterson and they pushed me under the seat and sat on me and I still cheered for you and they said they'd throw me over the gallery, but they couldn't really. I didn't care.'

'At the *swimming* gala?' What had she got to do with the swimming gala? Penn was puzzled, adrift.

'I go to Parkside.'

'To school?'

That this little, perfect, poised, painted fragile bit of what Maxwell called crumpet was still a schoolgirl astonished Penn. She had no more in common with the Rita Fairweathers of the Beehive than he had with the Major Harmsworths of the world.

'But why didn't you say, last Saturday – say—?' Penn stumbled, unable to follow the workings of the female mind. On Wednesday she had cheered him in the swimming gala to such an extent that the rest of the school had sat on her, yet the following Saturday she had given him nothing but cool smiles and said she had liked his hair better the way it was before. What sort of logic was that?

'I was too shy,' she said, 'in front of Colin and them. But now it's all right. You don't think I'm awful, coming?'

Penn was in no fit state to pass comment on his own feelings. No words he knew could describe such confusion. By the time he became conscious of his surroundings again they were on the High Street, and his sexual appetite was overwhelmed by the purely practical craving for food, as the smells of hamburgers, fish and chips and coffee steamed out of the neon-lit doorways.

'Have you any money?' he asked, desperate. 'I didn't know – I'm sorry, but I haven't a penny. I left it in the pocket of my jeans when I changed—' 'It' was a solitary florin and three sixpences, the bus fare to Northend.

Sylvia searched in her handbag. 'One and threepence.'

Penn's heart sank to join his empty stomach.

'We'll buy a coffee and a bun,' she said, heading into a smoochy coffee bar with a jukebox accompaniment and tables in confidential little cubicles, 'and share it.'

Penn, trying not to dwell on the fact that one and threepence worth of chips would have suited him a lot better, followed her and gave the order. While they waited she said to him, 'Why are you wearing such peculiar clothes?' and he told her the story of his strange, disjointed day.

Back on the river at Fiddler's End, Major Harmsworth,

twiddling the knob of his transistor in search of the Aldeburgh Festival came upon a local news programme. 'Drama came to Moorham this afternoon when local schoolboy, John Bates, rowed up to the quay with the unconscious body of fifty-eight-year-old amateur fisherman, Mr Edwin Crocker, lying in his boat. Mr Crocker had suffered a heart attack while out fishing, and young Bates, passing in his own boat, saw him and went to his aid. Unable to lift the unconscious man on board his own boat, he rowed him back to Moorham. Police say he undoubtedly saved the life of Mr Crocker, who was rushed to Northend General Hospital in a critical condition. Bates, on being congratulated on his presence of mind, said, "There was nothing else I could do."'

Major Harmsworth said to Humphrey, 'Well, I'm glad to hear some of these kids can do the decent thing. One is apt to think that they're all the same type as that yobbo we picked up this afternoon. Never so much as a thank you!'

The announcer's voice continued: 'The Open Pianoforte competition which concluded Northend's Music Festival this afternoon in the Town Hall was won by the youngest competitor, Patrick Pennington, a pupil at the Beehive Secondary Modern School, from a record entry of fifteen.'

'How very strange!' said Humphrey. 'You said that yobbo's name was Pennington – or am I getting mixed up?'

'Yes, his name is Pennington. Some relation perhaps.'

'But he said something about playing in a competition in Northend when he left us.'

'Good God, man, ping-pong or some such! Ah, this is it. The flute concerto by Leclair . . .'

Penn drank half a cup of coffee from the opposite side to the large silver lipstick marks, and ate half the dried-up bun which fell into his empty stomach like a pebble into a bucket. He did not know whether his hallucinatory state of mind was due to Sylvia or hunger.

'I could have died when I found out you were still at school,' she said. 'I thought you were nineteen or something.'

Penn, having thought Sylvia was above such Rita Fairweather-type remarks, contracted slightly, and stared into the coffee cup.

'I didn't think you were at school either.'

'Well, I'm leaving next month. I'm going to be a hairdresser. What are you going to do?'

Cripes, that was a question and a half! Apart from going to Oakhall for three months, he had no more idea now than he had when he was in his pram. He could not understand why, with Sylvia in front of him, admiration shining from her fantastic eyes, he felt these cold areas of despair touching him again.

'Drive a lorry or something, I suppose, if I'm lucky.'

'Can you drive?'

'Yes.' There was an old car on the farm that he and Bates had learned to drive on, progressing from tractors.

'But everyone wants to drive a lorry,' he said gloomily.

And no one was going to want a lorry driver with Oakhall on his record.

'What shall we do?' Sylvia said.

Penn could scarcely believe it, but when she said that, he had a yearning to be at home, curled up in bed, out of the world. He would even have found comfort in his parents quarrelling, and Mrs Jones hammering on the wall, and his father slamming out to the pub. He crushed the thought, and made a move to depart.

'Shall we walk along the front?' she said. 'Or we could go home? I only live ten minutes away. Would you like that? My parents won't mind.'

A brief picture slipped through Penn's mind of a comfortable sofa, the lights dimmed for television, the parents out – or possibly the mother out in the kitchen preparing a great big meal – and Sylvia's hand in his as it had been before the interruption for coffee.

'Yes. All right,' he said.

They got up and went outside. Sylvia came up close and put her arm round him inside the Major's Aran jersey, so that it lay on the bare flesh of his midriff. Penn felt the hair rise up on the back of his neck exactly as it had when Mr Crocker had opened his eyes in the bottom of the boat. Cripes, he thought, what doesn't she know? Yet she kept on walking, and chatting away, as if she thought it made no difference to him at all: the effect of her four fingers and thumb spread over his right-side bottom floating rib. It occurred to him then that she was, in fact, unaware of the feelings she aroused. She was talking about hairdressing. He was wildly indignant, not listening, thinking of all the things they said about girls at school, and how right they were, how unfair it all was. It was always the boys that got into trouble for taking advantage, but no one ever said how the girls led you on, with their eyes looking and their dresses showing everything . . . how was a boy supposed to know what on earth they wanted? And then afterwards it was all easy for girls, too. They could get any old job, and stop as soon as they got married in a year or two, and live on somebody else's money with their feet up watching the telly, while the poor bloke was at work all day. He put his arm up and touched her, moved by this indignation, and she pulled away and said,

'Hey, who do you think you are?' Then she giggled. The injustice of it! The disturbing hand dropped and held his own and they walked on in silence. Penn was soothed. Girls spoilt everything when they talked. They had no idea. He hoped her house wasn't much farther. His damp feet were cold as clams and all shrivelled up like toad's skin.

'Here we are,' she said.

The house was smart, tarted-up Northend early Victorian, pink-washed stucco and converted penthouse looking out into the sky. Penn was put off by the smell of affluence, until Sylvia said, 'We don't own it, for heaven's sake! Just a flat. My dad's the caretaker.' She let herself in with her own key and shouted, 'Mum! I'm back! I've got a friend.'

They were watching the telly, but got up far more brightly than his own parents would have done in the same circumstances, and switched it off. Penn was impressed by such manners, and self-conscious about Major Harmsworth's seventeen-inch trouser legs. Sylvia introduced him, and explained about the clothes, and told her parents all about the Folk Festival, only nothing about coming home early for the reason she had told Penn. Penn was invited to sit down, not on the sofa, but on a fireside chair with wooden arms. Sylvia's mother sat on the sofa next to Sylvia, and her father sat opposite

Penn looking slightly gloomy and obviously wondering how the Saturday night play had been going to finish. Sylvia's mother was a well-preserved, carefully made-up, very friendly little woman, her father the type that was used to never getting a word in edgeways, and who had opted for the line of least resistance. He looked at Penn with a cautious, faintly sympathetic expression on his face, as if sorry for him for getting involved with the same women who had defeated him long ago. Sylvia, throwing off her coat, revealed the same silvery, very short dress that had so fascinated Penn before. Seeing her now, so close and yet quite unattainable, in the presence of her parents, Penn was overcome by a sense of opportunities lost: when he could have got somewhere with her, just now, if he had been smooth and cunning, when they were alone, he had wasted all his time getting indignant and fuming away about girls having all the luck. Now, because he could not touch her, he had only to look at her to feel his desire to touch her rising up inside him, expanding like an awakening chrysalis. He pulled his eyes away and looked at her father instead.

Sylvia's mother said, 'And what do you do, Patrick?'

'He plays the piano,' Sylvia said. 'Not just like most people do, but properly, just like – like—' She hunted round to think up the name of a famous pianist, in vain, and said, 'Like Yehudi Menuhin plays the violin.'

Cripes! thought Penn, looking at the floor and going scarlet. He wanted to sink.

'He's just won the class at the festival. I went to hear him. He's absolutely marvellous. Go on, Pat, play that thing you played at the festival for Mum and Dad. Mum's ever so keen on the piano. She plays, but nothing like you do.'

'Oh, yes, dear, how lovely! Do play for us! I used to play in all the festivals when Sylvia was a little girl. My word, how I love it!'

Penn, wanting to die, looked up and saw to his horror that not only was there a piano in the room but Sylvia's mother had got to her feet and was opening it up and moving a pile of knitting off the stool. He could not believe the magnitude of his bad luck.

'You haven't got to,' Sylvia's father said.

'Oh, but of course!' Sylvia's mother contradicted. 'Why, it's years since this old piano was used properly! Although we always have the tuner in every six months, so it's quite all right. Come along, dear. Do play for me! Why, I can't imagine any way I'd rather spend an evening!'

Penn said, desperate, 'It's rather a noisy piece. The people upstairs—' Shades of Mrs Jones.

'Oh, but my dear, he *can't* complain! He's a piano

teacher himself. We spend hours listening to his terrible little boys and girls, so he really can't say a word.' She laughed delightedly. 'There, you've no excuse, has he, Sylvia?'

Sylvia laughed, too. Penn set his teeth. He could never have imagined such treachery. He got up and went over to the piano without another word. He played the Andante and Rondo Capriccioso with what felt like his last remaining strength and when he thundered up and down the double octave scales at the end of the piece, a photograph of a wedding-group on the mantelpiece fell flat on its face, teetered and dropped into the hearth. The glass broke, and Penn was fiendishly pleased.

'Oh, my word, but that was splendid!' said Sylvia's mother, her face glowing with admiration. 'Gracious me, but no one's ever played this old piano like that before! Oh, my dear, if only I'd kept it up . . . Get up a minute, dear. All my music is in the stool. Let's have a look at it, and perhaps you could play some of my favourites for me? What's the thing by Chopin that I used to spend so much time on, Henry? Do you remember? Look, what have we here?' She was scrummaging and rummaging, pulling out piles and piles of music which she laid all over the floor. 'Oh yes. Here, Patrick. Look, do you know this one? Oh, how I love that thing! I don't think anything more lovely has ever been written . . . Sit down, dear, and play it through for me.'

Penn sat down, taking the music with a feeling not of wanting to die, but having died. The music was an unrecognizable version of the Polonaise in A major, emasculated into beginner's fudge. He put it on the rack and started to play the real thing, and he played it with a passion that was in reality pure rage. The effect was magnificent, the best he had ever played it, even with Crocker standing over him. When he had finished, the rage had died out, and an unfamiliar little quirk of elation touched him, just as when he had finished the competition and had known he had played well. He had stretched himself, and been surprised by what he could do. He was very happy and did not want to stop, and went straight on into one of the nocturnes, while Sylvia's mother was still saying, 'My word, but it never sounded like that when I played it!' After the Chopin he played Beethoven's Pathétique Sonata and three of Mendelssohn's Songs without Words, and the first movement of the Moonlight Sonata, and two Chopin preludes, a waltz, and a Mozart study.

When he got up from the piano the room was very quiet. He stood, yawning. The fire was out, and Sylvia and her mother had gone. Henry was stretched out in his armchair, fast asleep. The hands of the clock on the mantelpiece had passed midnight. Penn closed the piano and Henry opened his eyes and said, 'You beat 'em, Patrick. They went to bed half an hour ago. Well done, boy. You can sleep on the sofa, if you want.' Penn shook his head, and went to the front door and let himself out, closing it silently behind him. The cold sea air came to him, cooling the sweat beneath the Aran jersey, rattling the dead laburnum blossoms and the rusting lilac, blowing the sweet papers along the gutter. Penn put his hands in Major Harmsworth's pockets and walked along, aimlessly, in the direction of the front. Then, still strung up by the music, he thought of Mr Crocker, and turned up the next street which led to the hospital. He had to tell old Crocker, and he had forgotten all about it. He did not know what would please Crocker most, that he had won the competition or that he had played for three hours because he wanted to and not because he had been told to. His hands burned as if they were on fire, but all the rest of him shivered, and the self-pity gnawed as strongly as the hunger. His mind was full of Oakhall, but he was so hungry he kept thinking of the baked beans and the thin stew and the bread and marge, and they were so desirable that he began to wish he were already there. He felt stoned, like Henry in the armchair, washed up on the sea of noise that he had wrung from the upright Bluthner with the wrought-brass candle-holders, which had dispersed the women and broken the picture-glass. He walked warily, an eye for the prowling copper.

When he came to the hospital, he went to the Casualty door out of force of habit (having had to present himself there on various occasions on what Maxwell called their 'après-soccer evenings', after particularly hard-fought matches), and when he found out his mistake, he was too tired to go away, but sat down on the nearest chair.

A brisk young nurse came out and said, 'What's wrong with you, then?' And then, 'Why, hullo, Pat. I thought the soccer season was over?'

Penn recognized a particularly nice nurse who had defended him once when a Soggy-minded sister had given him a jab for tetanus which had evoked from him a bellow that had woken up the whole slumbering ward. (The nice nurse had said the needle was blunt enough to shame a veterinary surgeon specializing in rhinoceros disease, and the sister had blasted her out for her impudence with invective worthy of Soggy himself; after that, he and the nurse had become very friendly.)

'Hullo,' he said. 'I'm visiting. I'm all right.'

'Our visiting hours are two to three-thirty in the afternoon, not in the early morning,' she pointed out.

'Have you got anything to eat?' he asked. 'I'm starving.'

She went off and came back with a solitary currant bun. 'Nurse O'Brien's slimming. You're lucky. Now then, what's the trouble?'

Penn explained. 'The point is, I think he got ill because of – of things that happened, to do with me, and things I said that worried him. But now I've won this old competition it might cheer him up quite a lot. It doesn't mean much really, but it does to him. He's a bit cracked that way. I just thought he ought to know.'

'I'll ring through,' she said. 'They'll never let you see him this time of night.'

She picked up the telephone, and after a good deal of back-chat and giggling, she said to Penn, 'Now then. What was the message?'

'Just say Pennington played in the competition and won it.'

The nurse passed it on. 'For Mr Crocker,' she said. 'There you are,' she said to Penn. 'Message delivered. He's asleep at the moment, but they'll tell him when he wakes up.'

'He's all right?'

'He's not all right, but not expected to die.'

Penn felt enormously relieved, in a way that surprised him. Almost as if everything was all right, as if he even wasn't going to Oakhall, and wasn't stranded in Northend without a penny, dying of starvation and nowhere to go.

'I'm ever so glad,' he said.

The nurse looked at him curiously. 'I thought you hated all schoolteachers?'

'Nearly all. Not him. I suppose you haven't got a spare bed in here?'

'Not for healthy specimens like you. Go out and get run over, and I'll see what I can do.'

He went out and down the drive. At the bottom there was a car park with three cars in it. Penn tried the doors, and the third one, an Austin 1100, was unlocked and had the key in the ignition, as if the whole thing was meant. Penn got in and sat in the driving-seat. He thought he would drive himself as far as the Wagon and Horses, a mile and a half from home, and leave the car in the car park there, and no one would connect it with him. He wouldn't be fool enough to drive it right to Fiddler's End. Then it occurred to him that there was no particular reason why he had to drive home at all. If the car had enough petrol in it, he could drive anywhere he chose, and when Mitchell came knocking for him, he wouldn't be there, and nobody in the whole wide world would know where he had to go. He switched on the ignition and started the engine, to get the petrol gauge registering. The needle went right up to Full. Penn switched off again, and went on sitting there. It was as if providence had provided. What difference would it make, he wondered, because they were putting him away anyway? A nurse walked past him down the drive, and didn't even give him a glance. Stealing a car was so easy it was criminal to take advantage of it. He sat back in the seat, fiddling with the lever to give himself more leg room, wondering where to go. Everywhere seemed rather pointless. He knew, even then, that he wasn't going to go anywhere, because if he had meant to, he wouldn't have switched the engine off after he had seen the petrol gauge so encouragingly full. He was just too hidebound, father-fixated, Mitchell-hounded, Stacker-nagged, Soggy-beaten, to have the guts left to run away. He could have cried, the way he felt.

He got out of the car and walked back up the drive to the ambulance shed, where two men were playing cards in a little room. Crombie's father was an ambulance man, and Penn asked them if they knew him, and after a bit, when they were quite friendly, he asked them if they'd let him bed down in the shed until it was light. They gave him an old stretcher that was out for repairs, and a red blanket, and he lay down and went to sleep.

CHAPTER TWELVE

AT EIGHT-THIRTY the following morning an extremely considerate woman in Fiddler's End started labour pains, and the ambulance men gave Penn a lift home on the way to collect her. He arrived outside his own front gate at nine o'clock. A pale blue Austin Princess was parked outside, which he studied suspiciously. It did not look like a police car. Penn went in at the kitchen door, uncertain of what to expect.

His father was in the kitchen, reading the *News of the World* and drinking tea. He looked up and said, 'Oh, so you've decided to come home?'

'Who's here?' Penn asked. He could hear his mother talking to someone in the living room.

'Some bloke asking for you. I thought it was a plain-clothes man, but it isn't. You know the coppers are looking for you?'

'Bates said.'

'I thought you'd scarpered.'

Penn shrugged.

His father said, 'It might come easier for you if you go down to the station. I'll take you down on the bike when I'm ready.'

'All right. Anything to eat?'

'I've had mine. What you wearing, for Pete's sake?'

'I got wet, I borrowed these. Who's this bloke, then?'

'Search me. Go and ask him. He looks like a blooming parson.'

Penn frowned. He looked in the pantry for something to eat, in vain, took a handful of raisins out of the jar on the shelf and went upstairs. He didn't want to face any old parson in Major Harmsworth's get-up. The sooner his mother stopped yapping and cooked him some breakfast the better he'd be pleased. He washed, scrummaged in the airing cupboard for some clothes, and went downstairs combing his hair. His mother, hearing him, came out of the living room and said, 'Oh, Pat, wherever have you been? There's a gentleman here interested in your playing. Come and speak to him.' She looked agitated, and slightly out of her depth. Penn said, 'What playing?' undecided between soccer and the piano, and then, urgently, 'I'm starving, Mum. Can't I have some breakfast?'

His mother, ignoring him, put her head into the living room and said, 'He's here, Mr – er—' She took Penn by the arm and shoved him bodily into the room.

A man was standing in front of the empty hearth, wearing a weary expression which Penn guessed had been brought about by too much of his mother. The man confirmed this by saying, with a touch of asperity, 'Can I speak to him alone for a few minutes?'

'Go in the front room, then. You'll be comfortable in there.'

She opened the other door and gave Penn another shove in its direction. The man followed, and shut it behind him decisively. Penn looked at him without saying anything, his face cold. It could only be trouble. The man had an air of authority that Penn could sense instinctively; it was much stronger than any he had yet come across, and Penn was a connoisseur of people in authority. He was about forty-five, tall, well-dressed, and extremely sure of himself, with a look in his eyes that commanded respect. Penn felt distinctly uneasy.

'My name is Hampton, Professor Hampton,' he said. 'I heard you play the piano last night.'

Penn was not cheered by the news.

'At the competition?'

'No, at a house in Laburnum Avenue.' The man explained: 'I was staying with an old fellow student of mine – I've been in Northend for a few days judging the part-singing and the school choirs. This friend has a flat in Laburnum Avenue, one up from where you were giving a recital last night. We heard you through right to the end — we had no choice, in fact — flats being what they are. This morning we inquired as to your name and looked up your address in the entries for the festival.'

'I wasn't giving a recital,' Penn said, wanting to get the facts straight. 'The old girl there wanted me to play. She didn't give me any choice.'

'Were you playing what she asked for?'

'I just played all the stuff I knew.'

'Who teaches you?'

'Mr Crocker at school.'

'Crocker? Edwin Crocker?'

'Yes, I think he's Edwin.'

'That's interesting. I knew him once. Used to play first flute in the Academy orchestra, very sound man. Well, isn't that strange?' He looked pleased. Penn was bored, wanting his breakfast.

Hampton said, 'You're not in a hurry, I hope?'

'I've got all day.' (Apart from an appointment at the police station.)

'How old are you?'

'Nearly seventeen.'

'When are you leaving school?'

'Next month.'

'What are your plans? Where are you going to study?'

Penn nearly said Oakhall, but stopped in time. He looked at Hampton suspiciously. 'What do you mean, study?'

'Do, then. What are you going to do?'

'Get a job.'

'At what?'

The same old question. 'Drive a lorry or something.'

'What about your music?'

'Well, what about it?'

They stared at each other, Penn on the defensive against this unexpected probing. He wasn't at the police station yet. When the man's gaze did not leave him, Penn looked away, worried. What was it all about?

'Look,' said the man. 'Sit down here and play me something. Whatever you're studying. Your choice.'

Penn sat down and played the Minute Waltz, the shortest piece he could think of. Hampton watched him intently. When he had finished he asked him for scales and arpeggios in several keys, and asked him to play a piece of Bach which he provided out of his briefcase, and a piece Penn had never set eyes on before, and to play a Mozart duet with him, also provided out of the briefcase. Penn's suspicions settled into a baffled resignation.

'Go and look out of the window,' Hampton said next. 'Tell me what key I'm playing in.'

Penn went. Bates was coming down the street, looking very cheerful, making for the Penningtons' front gate.

'B flat,' he said.

'What modulations am I making?'

'C major to B flat major . . . to E flat . . . F minor . . .' Bates saw Penn standing in the window and stood on the path making incomprehensible signs.

'What is the middle note of this chord?'

Bates mouthed, 'Did you win?'

'F sharp,' Penn said, and nodded his head at Bates.

'This one,' Hampton said.

Bates clasped his hands over his head and started prancing about until he got hooked up in a rose bush.

'E,' said Penn.

'And this?'

'C sharp.'

'What?' mouthed Bates. He came close to the window, and peered in, flattening his nose on the glass.

'Intervals?' said the Professor.

'Fifth . . . augmented fourth . . . diminished fifth . . . major ninth . . .' Penn mouthed at Bates, 'Clear off!'

'Who's he?' Bates said, rolling his eyes towards the Prof.

'God knows,' Penn said, shrugging his shoulders.

'I beg your pardon?' said the Professor.

'Minor seventh,' Penn said.

'Very good indeed,' said the Professor. 'Come here.'

Penn put out his tongue to Bates, and went back to the piano.

'Play me the piece you played for the competition. Mendelssohn, wasn't it?'

Penn scowled. There was a smell of frying bacon creeping under the door, which made him feel faint.

'Now?' he asked mutinously.

The Professor just looked at him, without a word, and Penn sat down and played the Andante and Rondo Capriccioso. When he had finished he found his father was standing in the doorway watching him. As soon as the last chord faded, his father said, 'Look, this is all very well, but if those coppers come up here, Pat, and find you monkeying about on the piano when I know they want you, I'll get into trouble as well as you.'

'It's me that's monkeying about on the piano, as you put it,' the Professor said. 'What are you talking about – coppers? What's wrong?'

'They want him,' said Mr Pennington. 'They've been wanting him since Friday night. They're going to book him for riding a motorbike uninsured.'

'Oh, is that bad?' Hampton said.

'Well, it is for him, seeing as they gave him his last chance the time before last, so to speak.'

'Why, does he do it often?'

'He does other things as well,' Mr Pennington said heavily. 'It's not always that. They've got it in for him, that's all.'

Hampton looked at Penn, who felt humiliated. But he could not deny the charge.

'What's likely to happen to him? This time, I mean?'

Don't mind me, Penn thought. Just carry on talking.

'He'll get three months.'

'How extraordinary!' said Hampton. He looked at Penn as if he were a new species. Penn didn't see his reasoning.

'Do you mind?' he said to Penn.

'Yes, of course I mind.'

'Why did you do it, then?'

'I wanted to get somewhere in a hurry.' Afterwards, when it was too late, he thought he could have added, 'To play the piano.'

The Professor looked at his watch. 'Would it help if I drove you to this police station, wherever it is? Would you mind if I came along?'

Penn shrugged. 'I don't mind.'

'Go and put a tie on,' his father said. 'We might get you out of it if we say the right things. Yes, sir, no, sir.'

Penn went upstairs and his father followed him up, while the Professor went outside to turn his car round.

'What's he want?' Mr Pennington asked Penn. 'Who is he, for Pete's sake, sticking his nose in?'

'Search me. You said he was the vicar,' Penn said crossly. 'Giving me a blooming examination this time of day! Aren't I going to get any breakfast? I shall die!'

'Doesn't look like it. Start dying.'

Penn groaned, and thudded downstairs again. They went out of the front door and out to the waiting Professor. Bates came round from the kitchen door and said to Penn, 'I say, I wanted to talk to you. Where you going?'

'Can't you guess?' Penn said gloomily.

'Oh, look, I say, I must talk to you before you get done. Is there room for me?'

'Yes, get in,' said the Professor.

The more the merrier, thought Penn. Take me to the graveyard and lay the sod o'er me. He and Bates got in the back of the car, and as the Professor drove out of the village, Bates said, 'You won, you said?'

'Yes.'

'I knew you would! That was some day! Do you know, I sang, and someone asked me and Colin if we'd go and perform at some old party. For money! And there's a group in Tolchester who asked if I would sing with them at some do or other next month. I mean, that was a good old day, wasn't it, you winning, and my career all starting up like that?'

And mine, Penn thought gloomily. 'Yes,' he said.

'Oh, and look, this thing I really want to tell you.' Bates hesitated, and looked stricken. 'I couldn't help it, Penn. I don't know what you'll say. About this old rescue thing yesterday – Mr Crocker—'

'What about it, then?'

'Well, there was quite a fuss when I got back there. You know, quite a crowd gathered, and they asked what had happened and everything, and a man came from a newspaper, and the ambulance and – and they all made quite a fuss. Of me, I mean.' His voice dropped. 'And when I got back last night, Mum said somebody had been round saying something about me being put up for some old medal or something. Something about a Humane Society.'

Penn said nothing.

'Do you mind?' Bates said nervously.

'Why should I?' Penn said, choked.

'You know why.'

'Well, what am I supposed to do?'

'I'm sorry, Penn. I told them it wasn't me, all of it, but you know, they get it all wrong. I suppose I didn't say it properly. I could've died when Mum said about a medal. I thought if you were to come and see this bloke, whoever he is, you could say it should be you.'

Penn flamed up. 'I don't want a stinking old medal, do I? What good's it to me, where I'm going? Ruddy great medal hanging round my neck! Don't talk such stupid crap, Bates.'

'Oh, Penn, I'm terribly sorry.'

'Shut up, Bates. You make me sick.'

'Oh, listen, Penn. That bird, the one you're stuck on, did you see her last night? She asked me where you were.'

'Yes, I saw her. She took me home with her and I had to play the ruddy piano for her mother all night.'

'Well, what d'you expect? I hope it put you off her.'

'Yes, it did.'

'Good.'

The conversation had run its natural course, and they were in Moorham, coming up to the police station. The Professor had been talking to Mr Pennington all the way, but what about, Penn had no idea. They all got out and went inside. Bates had second thoughts as soon as he got inside the door and said, 'I must be dreaming!' He turned sharply to make a retreat, but Sergeant West had seen him and called out, 'Stay with us, Bates!' Bates groaned.

The Professor went up to West and said, 'May I have a word with you, in private?'

'Yes, sir,' West said in a tone of voice which made Penn think that he, too, recognized an air of authority when he met it. West opened the door to the interrogation chamber and said to Mr Pennington, 'If you'll just wait in here with the boys – I'll be right with you.'

They filed in and the door shut.

'You are a damned fool, Pat,' Pennington said to his son. 'Getting sent down for a damn-fool thing like this.'

'I've nothing else to do for the next three months,' Penn said savagely.

'Well, I don't know,' his father said. 'That bloke – what's his name? – said he'd like you to go up to London to some place or other. I've forgotten the name he said. Wouldn't cost us anything, he said. I said if it did, I wouldn't be interested.'

'What are you talking about? To do what?'

'To play the piano. He said you'd get a grant, a scholarship, or something.'

Penn was furious. 'Me? Are you raving? *Me?* Go to a twit house full of pianists! He never said that!'

'Who are you telling? He did say it.'

'He must be ruddy daft! I'm no good for that sort of thing. He ought to ask Crocker if I'm any good. Ask Soggy! If I am, they've been keeping it ruddy dark all this time.'

'You won that competition, didn't you?' Bates said.

'Yes, from a lot of old women. That doesn't count for anything, does it?'

'What competition?' Mr Pennington asked.

Penn scowled, shaken to the marrowbone. He sat down and laid his arms across the table, feeling quite weak.

'I thought it was a bit funny myself,' his father said. 'But he didn't seem to be joking. I'll ask him again afterwards, if he's still around.'

'Nosey old beggar,' Penn said. 'Interfering.'

Whatever it was the nosey old beggar had to say to West, it seemed to take some time. Penn could hear their voices without being able to distinguish what they were saying. He didn't care for being discussed, like a thing; what little command he had ever had of his own fate seemed to have crumbled away completely during the last few weeks. He was utterly exhausted, like a wet sock, and as useless. He dropped his head on his arms and shut his eyes.

West put his head round the door.

'Mr Pennington, we want a word with you.'

His father went out, grumbling, but Penn did not move. The voices went on, with Mr Pennington's indignation added for dramatic effect. Bates got up and stood by the door, straining his ears, but the police station doors had been built to frustrate just such contingencies.

'They're cooking up something horrible for you, Penn. West is going to book you for driving the piano too hard.'

Penn was not amused.

'I'm sorry, Penn,' Bates said miserably. 'Really, about everything.'

He leaned against the door, watching Penn, until the door jerked him in the shoulder-blades and West's voice hailed him crisply:

'Come on, you two, jump to it!'

He got out of the way and West, with a jerk of his head, beckoned them outside. Penn dragged himself mutinously to his feet. His father was standing outside the door, looking dazed and slightly apprehensive.

'Pat, it's all right,' he said. 'You've got off.'

West eyed Mr Pennington sternly.

'Tell him the whole story. There are conditions.'

'Pat, listen to this. Mr Hampton – the Professor here – wants you to go up to London somewhere and study with him. Won't cost us anything – he says you'll get a grant or a scholarship or something. Sergeant West says if you go, he'll let you off.'

'Oh, come, Mr Pennington, I didn't put it quite like that. I said, "Let the boy think it over." Professor

Hampton here wants to take him out for lunch, for a little chat. I said it's Mitchell that wants to arrest him, and Mitchell isn't around just at the moment, as fortune might have it. And if, over lunch, the Professor is able to talk Patrick here into doing something sensible with his life, who knows that I won't be able to talk Mitchell into dropping this nonsense about a motorbike?'

Penn, seeing himself delivered from one academy of forced labour straight into the bosom of another, felt the indignation well up like water from a burst main. He opened his mouth to protest, but saw the room going round him in a most peculiar manner, and the words hadn't the strength to even fall, let alone explode, from his lips.

West hastily pushed him on to a chair and shoved his head down between his knees.

'Go and get a glass of water,' he said to Bates.

Mr Pennington said angrily, 'You ruddy police! Hounding him, that's what you've been doing! No wonder the kid—'

Penn's voice came faintly from the floor. 'I don't want water. I'm ruddy starving! I want my breakfast.'

The Professor laughed.

'Breakfast! I've already made my offer. If you pull yourself together, I'll take you down to the Swan for lunch.'

'It's a good offer, Pat,' said West. 'The whole deal. Come on, you think about it.'

He waved a file of papers about under Penn's nose, and Penn got uncertainly to his feet. The Professor moved forward and took his elbow, and Penn found himself propelled smoothly out of the room, across the outer room and into the street. The wind off the river, bringing spray and ooze and mud and freedom, restored his equilibrium. He leaned against the wall for a moment, not quite sure what was happening. The Professor stood regarding him with a certain amount of sympathy.

'Don't think I'm presuming to order your life for you. I just chatted up the sergeant. I take it you don't want to be – how do they phrase it? – sent down for three months?'

'No. But I don't—' He hesitated, looking into the Professor's steely eye. 'I don't know what . . .'

The Professor worried him. He knew that the Professor had got him off, with his private word in West's ear, and that the Professor was going to manipulate him, smoothly, and cleverly. He was another of them, telling him what to do. But the Professor was more clever than any of the others. Penn sensed it, and it frightened him. He knew he could neither despise nor disobey the Professor. He walked beside him in silence. The fact that he had got out of Oakhall meant very little beside the significance of what he had got into.

'What's the matter?' the Professor said. 'Apart from your being hungry, I mean? Which we shall soon put right. Is the idea of studying music seriously completely new to you?'

'Nobody's ever suggested it before, no.'

'Mr Crocker never suggested it?'

'No.'

'Why not? Do you know?'

'I suppose because—' Penn was not articulate enough to express what he felt. He could not explain to Hampton just what Crocker was up against, in their strange, closed world of frustrated effort; he could not tell Hampton what a pig he, Pennington, was; how he had driven Crocker nearly to death.

'I – I get into trouble. I don't work. They want me to leave. Tomorrow, if I go back, I shall get expelled for something I've done.' Even while he was speaking, he was amazed at what he was saying. As if it was a confessional or something. He must be more light-headed than he knew. The Professor opened the door of the Swan, and they went into the dining room, and the waiter took them to a table and pulled out the chairs for them. The Professor was the sort of man waiters did not ignore. The smell of roast lamb and roast beef and roast chicken made Penn feel faint again.

'I don't like playing the piano,' he said.

'Why did you play for three hours last night, then?'

'I started because that woman made me.'

'She kept on at you, for three hours?'

'No. Just to start. When I finished they were all in bed asleep.'

'Why, then?'

Penn did not know. 'I felt like it, I suppose.'

The Professor smiled.

Penn said angrily, 'There's no *pleasure* in it.'

'I should hope not indeed. The pleasure is for the audience. For you it's pleasure sometimes, but a good deal more of the old sweat and pain. I'm having the minestrone, I think. What about you?'

Penn took the menu. He wasn't going to win, so he might as well go down eating. Sweat and pain. The old geezer could say that again.

'Oxtail,' he said. 'And roast beef.'

'It would, of course, be a crime if you were to become a lorry-driver.'

'I've got to do something.'

'I'd like to take you on, you know. You would get a scholarship without any trouble. You'd live in a room in London, with enough money to get by on. You'd have to practise four or five hours a day and you'd have to go to some lectures and concerts which you might, conceivably, find interesting. The rest of the time would be your own.'

Penn was silent. The waiter brought the soup, and they both drank it without speaking. Penn ate three bread rolls with his, and the Professor's prospect seemed less impossible than it did on an empty stomach.

Just before the beef came he said, 'People like me aren't students.'

The Professor laughed. 'Don't be so Victorian! Underprivileged backgrounds are in, these days. Parents like yours are fashionable. Horseradish sauce, please,' he added to the waiter.

Penn was indignant, but immediately distracted by a large plate flowing with thin red rounds of beef and steaming gravy, and mounds of roast potatoes, peas, carrots and Yorkshire pudding. He started to eat, concentrating hard. When he had finished he saw no reason at all why he shouldn't be a student. After all, he was used to about three hours a day, and even if he didn't like it, he didn't like anything else better.

'I could try it,' he said cautiously.

The Professor smiled. 'I don't ask many people to study with me,' he said, very smoothly. 'Usually they ask me, and I turn them down.'

Take that, thought Penn. He knew when he had met his match. Oakhall would be nothing compared to what was opening up before him. Cold showers and press-ups would be as summer zephyrs beside the relentless pressures of Bach, Beethoven, and Brahms that hove on the horizon.

'I'll have the chocolate gateau,' he said to the Professor, who was offering him the menu again, 'with fresh cream. And a large coffee.'

Another five hundred calories or so, and he would be able to face it with equanimity.

The nurse said to Mr Crocker, 'There's a boy outside called Pennington who wants to see you. I said no, but he's very insistent.'

'I would like to see him,' Crocker said. 'He is the one person I want to speak to.'

'Only for a few minutes, then,' said the nurse.

Penn, looking very tidy and awed, appeared round the door and came slowly up to the bed.

'Hullo, Pennington.'

'I'm sorry, sir, if it was to do with me, you landing here. I had to come and say.'

'It was to do with Mr Marsh, Pennington. What he did, after all our work . . . even if you deserved it, I didn't.'

'It's what made me go and play in the competition,' Penn said.

Mr Crocker looked at Penn wonderingly. '*That's* what made you? But, of course, I see now! That's the way you work, Pennington. Of course! Like the long hair! Oh, my God, we must make sure he finds out, Pennington, why you won the competition! What a strange boy you are – but consistent, I'll give you that. And you won. But of course I knew you'd win!'

'And there's something else,' Penn said. 'A Professor Hampton. Do you know him?'

'Of course I know him. Everyone knows him. He's one of the finest teachers of pianoforte in the country.'

'Well, he's going to teach me.'

'He—?' Crocker could not find words. He stared. His complexion went through white, grey, blue, white, pink and bright red. Penn got up in horror, thinking he had brought on another attack, and called the nurse.

'What is it?' she said, bustling in.

'Is he all right?' Penn asked.

'Yes, I'm all right, Pennington,' Mr Crocker said softly.

'What have you been doing?' the nurse said severely to Penn. 'He's not to have any excitement, I told you that.'

'Stop nagging,' said Mr Crocker. 'They're just like

someone we know, eh, Pennington? Always on at you.'

Penn smiled. 'Yes.'

'That's all very well, but what am I supposed to say
to the doctor when he looks at your chart? Now just say
goodbye, you,' the nurse said to Penn, 'and let him have
some rest.'

'Are you all right, sir?'

'Yes, Pennington. I've never been more all right in
all my life.'

'Well – er—' (The nurse had him by the arm and
was saying, 'Out.') 'Goodbye and – er – thank you and
all that—'

'Thank *you*,' said Mr Crocker.

'*Goodbye*,' said the nurse to Penn, and shut the door.

Penn, who always played the piano for assembly, finished
'Jerusalem', remembering just in time that it didn't have
an amen, and, while the school sat down with a din like
charging elephants and old Stacker shuffled his notes for
the week's announcements, he fished out 'Jesu, Joy of
Man's Desiring' ready for the dismissal. Maxwell was
leaning on the lectern behind him, having read the
lesson. Penn heard him yawn. He had told Maxwell and
company about getting off the motorbike charge, but he
hadn't told anyone about the Professor. The Professor
and his plans were something Penn felt he had to get

used to himself before he made the news public. It was something that came strangely; to be told that he was good was so uncommon that he had to chew it over to get the flavour, to reassure himself. He didn't, in fact, know if he could do what the Professor wanted, but he was willing to give it a try. He fancied living away from home, and he fancied very much being treated like a human being, which seemed to be the Professor's way. He liked the idea of telling Sylvia that he was going to college and coming down the odd weekend to take her out (but not home), possibly looking up old Crocker to report on progress. He liked the word student meaning hair whatever length he chose, and way-out clothes, and a room of his own in a comfortable house somewhere with no one to tell him what to do. For all this he was prepared to work quite hard.

These thoughts were going through his head while Stacker was giving out the notices. There was no point in his listening, because he knew immediately after assembly he was going to be expelled. He had seen two of the governors arriving in their cars. He didn't care a bit. Soggy was sitting in his usual place just below the platform, no doubt looking forward to the ceremony. He knew, for the whole school knew, that Penn had won the competition, but he had said nothing, and nobody in 5C had dared mention the subject to him.

Penn, watching Soggy, was suddenly aware by Soggy's expression of what Stacker was saying. Soggy's face had tightened up, the skull pressing out, the eyes glittering.

'. . . must congratulate him on winning the Open Pianoforte Competition in the Northend Music Festival . . . a great honour indeed for the school . . .' Nothing about the twelve stripes on the palms of his hands to help him on his way. Everyone was clapping and cheering except Soggy, who sat motionless.

When the noise had died down, Stacker said, 'I think it would be an appropriate moment, in view of this success, for Pennington to give us a short recital. Mr Crocker, unfortunately, is not here to conduct the choir in their usual Monday morning – er – piece, and, in view of the fact that Pennington will *very shortly* be leaving us, I feel we should take advantage of this opportunity to hear him play a few of the pieces he has been working on.'

Penn heard Maxwell give a snort of amusement behind him. His heart plummeted, a shot duck . . . He turned to Stacker.

'Now?' he asked angrily.

Stacker smiled sweetly. 'Yes, Pennington. Now.'

The old beggar was going to make him go out working. It was part of the punishment, the pre-expulsion aperitif, to get him sweating . . . He scowled furiously at Stacker.

'The competition piece first, and then perhaps that Chopin thing that everyone likes?' Stacker, still smiling, sat down and leaned back in his chair, adjusting to a musical-appreciation expression. There was an expectant, dead silence. Penn waited a moment, hoping for some phenomenal act of God, like a gas explosion or an aeroplane crashing, to deliver him, but nothing happened and into the silence he was forced to inject the Andante and Rondo Capriccioso which now, having served its purpose, was beginning to bore him to tears; everyone else sat back staring into space, glad to have their time wasted. The injustice speared him.

The applause at the end was prolonged, Penn was sure, by the purely self-protective instinct to put off starting lessons. He sat gloomily, waiting, and Stacker came over and said: 'Very nice, Pennington. Now the Polonaise.'

Useless to say he wasn't in the mood, that he didn't want to play his favourite Polonaise for *him*. He just wanted to sit, staring into space, as he did every day between the musical items of the school assembly, letting it all go past like seaweed on the tide. But he had no alternative. He took his blazer off and dropped it on the floor. He thought, if Stacker asked him for another one after this, he would say his hands hurt too much.

He waited for a diminuendo in the school's shuffling and snuffling and coughing, rather to put off what he didn't want to do than to play the part of the concert pianist, and while he waited he decided he would play the Polonaise for Crocker, for the last time, willing it in the direction of Northend General Hospital. He would play it how Crocker liked it, not as fast and as loud as he liked it himself, and he would sustain himself by thinking that one day, if his luck held, old Stacker would have to pay to hear him play the Polonaise. He nursed this very pleasant thought until the silence was complete, and then turned his whole attention to the precise time values the piece demanded, forgetting resentment in the effort of vindicating dotty old Crocker for his absurd faith in him. It was Soggy he was showing, scorching him for his cheap sneers. He played it very well, as well as he had played it for Sylvia's mother, and the applause, when it came, was loud and enthusiastic. Penn, very satisfied, looked at the audience. He saw Soggy, sitting ten feet away, lift his hands and clap once, and put his hands down again on his knees. His face was like stone.

Stacker came over and said to Penn, 'Just one more, I think. Whatever you like.'

It was then that Penn had a quite marvellous idea.

'Yes, sir.'

Maxwell, who had been propping himself against the piano while Penn played, was surprised to see Penn smile, as if he was perfectly happy. Not a bit like when Stacker had said, 'Now the Chopin.' Penn sat waiting for the school to settle down again. He looked at Maxwell and said, softly, 'I'm going to play "Tannenbaum".'

Maxwell goggled.

'You're *not*! You wouldn't dare!'

'Want to bet?' Penn said.

Maxwell went stiff with horror, watching Penn. He thought Penn was having him on, but with Penn anything was possible. Penn sat very still, waiting for silence, then started to play.

Maxwell had heard Penn play 'Tannenbaum' several times, generally when he was in a bad temper, and he had always played it very loudly and angrily, but now – and Maxwell thought for a moment that Penn had been joking after all – the opening chords rippled off the keyboard as daintily as the Mendelssohn fairies. Maxwell watched Penn's hands, not daring to look at anything else, amazed less by their virtuosity than by their nerve. The melody, familiar to Maxwell in its honky-tonk version from the mangled bowels of the Common Room piano, swelled from the Bechstein with an authority that made it seem perfectly in order as a concert piece, very round and romantic. Penn's face was expressionless, watching the performance of his fingers as if nothing was meant. But to Maxwell the stately tune, growing gradually louder, with rebellious arpeggios starting to sing out under the left hand, was quite simply a shattering public statement of Penn's scorn for everything Soggy stood for – as explicit as speech. It was as if all the very best four-letter words were being delivered to Soggy from the platform, wrapped in exquisite form, insult through melody, denigration through apparent obedience to the whims of Mr Stack, who still sat smiling, oblivious of the messages quivering through the atmosphere.

That the whole school was not oblivious of Penn's meaning was only too obvious. Maxwell took a white glance into the body of the hall, and saw the faces transfixed with utter, incredulous delight. The tension came to him like electricity, as if the whole school had stood up. The eyes were alight, sparkling with malicious glee, nudges and squeaks passing up and down the rows like wind through corn. Maxwell felt the hall tremble.

'Cripes, Penn!' he whispered. 'He'll kill you.'

Soggy was sitting bolt upright, his eyes fixed on Penn. Maxwell could see the threads of his rage working in little flicks and tics round his jawbone and down his neck, his mouth twitched and the sides of his nostrils filled out and drew in with the emotion that Maxwell could see could not possibly be contained for much longer.

Penn smiled.

'He can't do anything,' he said. 'Not now.'

And the tune came up out of the Bechstein like thunder. Maxwell could see the muscles working all down Penn's arms through the white shirt, and the tendons standing out on the back of his hands like the strings up Soggy's neck. He started to grin. It was just too beautiful, impossible not to enjoy it, and the whole school started to stir, no longer able to contain the same fantastic pleasure. The beginnings of mass laughter came like the prelude to some gigantic sneeze, spitting and popping up from the floor in uncontrollable tiny explosions. Soggy got to his feet. He stepped forward and came to the platform, so that his waist was on a level with Penn's feet, hard on the pedals. The sweat stood out in beads on his forehead.

'Mr Stack, that is enough!' he cried out. His voice was out of control, like the school. The first genuine shriek of laughter burst out behind him. He swung round, hands clenched. Maxwell thought he was going to have a fit.

Stacker stood up, goggle-eyed, unaware of what was causing the unbelievable behaviour of the whole school before his very eyes. He looked at Soggy having public hysterics and, with a promptness born of panic, roared into the hubbub, '*Dismiss!*'

Penn, in mid-bar, withdrew his hands, adjusted the music on the rack before him and immediately started to play 'Jesu, Joy of Man's Desiring'. The whole school turned as one man, drilled by sheer habit, buzzing with glee.

'Silence!' Stacker roared.

The lines started to file out, obediently silent, but buoyant with suppressed excitement. Penn played serenely, his eyes on the music, his fingers working on the gently flowing triplets in sweet legato as if nothing had occurred between this and the Chopin.

Maxwell came and stood at his shoulder, watching his hands sadly.

'I wouldn't like to be you, Penn,' he said.

'It doesn't matter,' Penn said. 'I've got myself a job. I'm going.'

He turned over a page, and played on. He was supremely happy, and playing the Bach was as fitting a way to feel happy at that moment as any other he could think of. It was beautiful in its ordered sanity; it was unbothered, tranquil, unpetty, utterly controlled and of inspired perfection. He could not think of words to express it, but the feelings were like silk. He felt wonderful, and played with total concentration, content that this was what he was going to do. It had all come right, and the Bach was the most right thing of all.

Mr Stack came up behind him and said, heavily, 'When you've finished, Pennington, come to my room. We have several things to discuss, I think.'

'Yes, sir.'

And Bach, as if he had known, went on and on, and Penn played him right to the end, and what was going to happen afterwards he neither knew nor cared.

MORE CLASSICS
TO DISCOVER

From Random House Children's Publishers

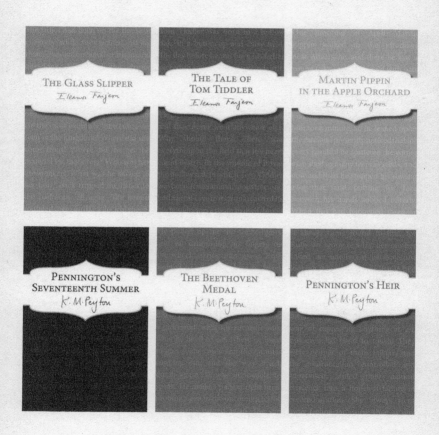

THE GLASS SLIPPER
Eleanor Farjeon

THE TALE OF
TOM TIDDLER
Eleanor Farjeon

MARTIN PIPPIN
IN THE APPLE ORCHARD
Eleanor Farjeon

PENNINGTON'S
SEVENTEENTH SUMMER
K. M. Peyton

THE BEETHOVEN
MEDAL
K. M. Peyton

PENNINGTON'S HEIR
K. M. Peyton

AVAILABLE IN EBOOK AND PRINT EDITIONS